W9-BHW-759

"We need to get out of here. Now."

"What happened?" Kate asked.

"A black car swept through the parking lot. I'm pretty sure the driver is one of Salvatore's men, looking for us."

"I'm ready," Kate whispered, coming over to stand beside Logan, so close he could feel the warmth of her arm against his.

It struck Logan that for the first time in months, he wasn't alone. There was someone to work with. Someone to bounce ideas off.

He couldn't fail her. Not the way he'd failed Jennifer. He refused to let Salvatore take another person from him.

Grimly he took Kate's arm and swept a glance over the parking lot to make sure there weren't any of Salvatore's goons around, before he hustled her out to his car, a nondescript sedan.

As he climbed into the driver's seat beside her, he silently vowed to do whatever it took to protect Kate.

No matter what the cost.

Books by Laura Scott

Love Inspired Suspense

The Thanksgiving Target
Secret Agent Father
The Christmas Rescue
Lawman-in-Charge
Proof of Life
Identity Crisis
Twin Peril
Undercover Cowboy

LAURA SCOTT

grew up reading faith-based romance books by Grace Livingston Hill, but as much as she loved the stories, she longed for a bit more mystery and suspense. She is honored to write for the Love Inspired Suspense line, where a reader can find a heartwarming journey of faith amid the thrilling danger.

Laura lives with her husband of twenty-five years and has two children, a daughter and a son, who are both in college. She works as a critical-care nurse during the day at a large level-one trauma center in Milwaukee, Wisconsin, and spends her spare time writing romance.

Please visit Laura at www.laurascottbooks.com, as she loves to hear from her readers.

UNDERCOVER COWBOY

LAURA SCOTT

HARLEQUIN® LOVE INSPIRED® SUSPENSE

If you purchased this book without a cover you should be aware that this book is stolen property. It was reported as "unsold and destroyed" to the publisher, and neither the author nor the publisher has received any payment for this "stripped book."

Recycling programs
for this product may
not exist in your area.

™ LOVE INSPIRED BOOKS

ISBN-13: 978-0-373-67555-5

UNDERCOVER COWBOY

Copyright © 2013 by Laura Iding

All rights reserved. Except for use in any review, the reproduction or utilization of this work in whole or in part in any form by any electronic, mechanical or other means, now known or hereafter invented, including xerography, photocopying and recording, or in any information storage or retrieval system, is forbidden without the written permission of the editorial office, Love Inspired Books, 233 Broadway, New York, NY 10279 U.S.A.

This is a work of fiction. Names, characters, places and incidents are either the product of the author's imagination or are used fictitiously, and any resemblance to actual persons, living or dead, business establishments, events or locales is entirely coincidental.

This edition published by arrangement with Love Inspired Books.

® and TM are trademarks of Love Inspired Books, used under license. Trademarks indicated with ® are registered in the United States Patent and Trademark Office, the Canadian Trade Marks Office and in other countries.

www.LoveInspiredBooks.com

Printed in U.S.A.

In their hearts humans plan their course,
but the Lord establishes their steps.
—*Proverbs* 16:9

This book is dedicated to my editor, Tina James.
Thanks for being so wonderful to work with!

ONE

"Kate, I'm in trouble," Angela Giordano, her former college roommate, whispered urgently through the phone. "You have to help me!"

Kate Townsend frowned and tried to ignore the churning in her stomach. She tightened her grip on the subway pole as the Chicago train lurched around a curve. "What kind of trouble?"

"I think my uncle is trying to kill me."

She sucked in a harsh breath, but couldn't say she was surprised. Angela's uncle was Bernardo Salvatore, suspected Chicago crime boss. "Why? What happened?"

"I can't tell you now," Angela whispered. "I need you to meet me here in the back of the restaurant. Hurry!"

No way was she going to the restaurant owned by Salvatore. Talk about walking straight into the lion's den. "Try to remain calm. I'll help you escape, but we have to meet someplace else." She tried to think logically. They needed to meet out in the open, in neutral territory. "I'm on the red line, heading north. Let's meet at Stanton Park. It's not far from the restaurant."

There was a long pause. "I'd rather wait for you to get here." Angela's voice had dropped so low Kate almost couldn't hear her. Had someone come outside to find Angela? Someone spying for her uncle? Salvatore wasn't the type to do his own dirty work.

"Stanton Park," Kate insisted, glancing at her watch. "I can meet you by the northeast corner of the building in forty minutes."

"Okay," Angela agreed, before quickly hanging up.

Kate clutched her phone, trying to calm her racing heart. She was worried about her former roommate, but she also hoped this might be the break she needed. Now that Angela was in danger, too, there was no reason for her to protect her uncle. Surely Angela would cooperate, giving the authorities inside information about Bernardo's activities.

And maybe, just maybe, Kate would find a solid link to her father's death. His murder. Her chest tightened painfully and the grief she'd tried so hard to keep at bay threatened to erupt.

She took several deep breaths, battling back the wave. She missed him so much. She still had trouble believing he was gone. The pastor at their church reminded her he was in a better place, but that knowledge didn't stop her heart from aching. Didn't stop her from crying herself to sleep at night.

From being determined to seek answers.

In the four weeks since her father's death, she'd become obsessed with trying to find a way to link Salvatore to the crash that had claimed her father's life. But she wasn't getting any help from official channels. According to the police report, her dad, a Chicago cop, had been on the way to the courthouse when he was killed in a motor vehicle crash. His driver's-side door was T-boned at a busy intersection. A witness had come forward claiming it was a tragic accident, and based on that statement, the cops were willing to close the case.

But Kate wasn't buying that story. For one thing, the driver of the other vehicle hadn't been hurt at all, and when she'd tried to track him down, it seemed as if he'd vanished without a trace. She couldn't find proof that a person with that name and address had ever existed. Also, she had thought it was suspicious that her father had died on the way to the courthouse to testify against Dean Ravden, one of Salvatore's goons. But since the only charge against Ravden was a DUI, no one believed that her father had been the victim of a mafia hit.

Not even her oldest brother, Garrett, who was also a Chicago cop. He'd listened patiently to her theory, but then told her she was imagining things.

Their father's unexpected death couldn't possibly be the result of a professional hit. Garrett told her the mafia wouldn't bother to stage a car accident— they would have simply shot him in the head. Or the heart.

Still, she knew deep down that somehow, some-way, Salvatore was responsible. With Angela's help, she might be able to prove it. Turning her grief into grim determination wasn't easy, but she steeled her resolve and focused on the upcoming meeting with Angie. It was nearly eight o'clock in the evening, which meant that it would be dark by the time she reached the park. She needed to arrange some sort of backup.

For a moment she considered contacting FBI Special Agent Logan Quail, but almost as soon as the thought formed, she rejected it. She'd only talked to Logan once in the six months since she'd been his informant while working as a waitress at Salvatore's restaurant. With his help, she'd left the mafia-owned restaurant without raising Salvatore's suspicions.

But once she'd recognized Dean Ravden during a news story, she'd called the number he'd made her memorize. Much like her brother, Logan had listened while she explained how she had seen Ravden meeting with Salvatore at the restaurant and why she thought her father was murdered. But while Logan thanked her for the information, he also told her in no uncertain terms to stay out of the investigation. He seemed distant and impatient with her for calling, so she simply agreed and hung up.

She shouldn't have been surprised at the way he'd shut her down, since Logan didn't think much of her goal to become a police officer. He'd made it clear he didn't believe women belonged in law enforcement.

During the few days they'd worked together, six months ago, she'd felt close to him, but once they were out of danger, he'd walked away. To be fair, he'd first tried to convince her to go into a safe house. When she refused, he left barely saying goodbye.

After Logan bruised her heart, she decided it was better to keep her distance. She'd thrown herself into her schooling, finishing up her criminal justice degree.

Being a cop was all she had ever wanted to do. Her grandfather, her father and her three older brothers were all in law enforcement. She'd intended to try out for the police academy, but then her father had died. And her world had spun out of control.

Now it was time to get back on track. She grimaced and pulled out her phone to call her eldest brother, Garrett. He hadn't believed her before, but surely he'd come through for her now that she had Angela as a potential witness. Maybe Angie could even verify that Ravden was one of her uncle's thugs.

For the first time in days, she felt a quiver of anticipation. She quickly dialed her brother and waited for him to answer.

"Katie? What's up?" Her brother's deep voice helped calm her nerves.

"I need your help. My old roommate Angela needs to get away from her uncle, Bernardo Salvatore. I'm heading over to meet her now. How quickly can you get to Stanton Park?"

"Are you crazy?" Garrett shouted in her ear, so loud she winced and pulled away the phone. "No way, absolutely not. It's too dangerous." Her brothers were always overprotective, but she couldn't remember the last time Garrett had yelled at her.

"But she might be able to give us key information," she pointed out, striving to remain calm. "I can stall until you get here."

"I'm more than an hour away and can't leave in the middle of my shift. Don't go, Kate. I mean it. I forbid you to go!"

Forbid? Since when did her brothers forbid her to do anything? She was so upset and shocked she could barely speak.

"Katie, please." Her brother's tone softened, as if he'd sensed he'd gone too far. "We'll meet her first thing in the morning, okay? Call her back and let her know we'll meet with her then."

"What if tomorrow is too late?" She knew only too well how Salvatore got rid of people. He murdered them in cold blood and then dumped their bodies into Lake Michigan. At least that's what he'd done six months ago, when a waitress at the restaurant had crossed him.

"Tell her we'll meet her later tonight then. I get off work in a couple of hours. Just don't meet her alone," her brother insisted.

"All right, I'll call her back." She hung up on her brother and then dialed Angie's number, but the call went straight through to voice mail.

She sighed and chewed her lip as she considered her options. Her brother didn't want her to meet Angela alone, but she wasn't helpless. She knew basic self-defense moves; her brothers had taught her well. She'd picked the location, not Angie. Therefore, she had the upper hand.

Again, she considered calling Logan Quail, but knew his reaction would be very similar to her brother's. She tried Angie one more time, and when she still didn't pick up, Kate decided she had no choice but to go to the park as planned. Her brother called, but she sent the call to voice mail. She didn't have time to argue with him, and besides, he was too far away to help her, which was why she'd called him in the first place.

When the subway stopped near the park, she elbowed her way past the crowds to exit the train.

Stanton Park wasn't far from Old Town, a short distance from Salvatore's restaurant. She walked quickly, avoiding direct eye contact with any of the other patrons.

She arrived at the park a good ten minutes early, and made sure she wasn't followed as she wound her way to the back of the park, where the recreation center was located. She'd thought a public place would be safe, but because of the late hour, there weren't many people around. Still, she rested against the side of the brick building before sending Angela a quick text.

I'm here. Where r u?

She waited a few minutes, but didn't get a response from Angela. Her stomach knotted with worry. First no response to her phone calls, and now no response to her text message. Had something happened? Had Salvatore or one of his men caught her at the restaurant before she could leave? Was Kate too late to help her?

Please, Lord, keep Angela safe.

Kate stood with her shoulder pressed against the brick wall, peering cautiously around the corner toward the front of the building, scanning the area. Her heart thudded painfully, as the seconds passed with agonizing slowness.

The area in front of the recreation center was

unusually quiet. Time passed slowly, until it was ten minutes past their arranged meeting time. She silently vowed to wait another ten minutes before heading back to the subway.

Then she saw Angela, dressed in the familiar Salvatore's waitress uniform of black skirt, black apron and crisp white blouse, walking briskly up the sidewalk toward the building. Kate let out her breath in a sigh of relief.

"Kate?" Angela called softly. "Where are you?"

For a moment she hesitated, the tiny hairs on the back of her neck lifting in sudden alarm, but before she could move the cold steel barrel of a gun pressed through into the center of her back. "Step forward very slowly," a low male voice said from behind her. "If you try to run, I'll shoot."

A trap! Stunned speechless, she could hardly wrap her mind around the fact that Angela had actually set her up. How else would the gunman have known she was here? Kate glared at her former roommate in horror as she followed the gunman's demand to take several steps forward.

Angela's eyes had widened in shock. "What are you doing? You promised you wouldn't hurt her!"

"Go back to the restaurant. This isn't your concern," the gravelly voice said. Battling her fear, she listened intently to the hint of an Italian accent in the gunman's voice. Her mouth went desert dry as she realized it wasn't likely Salvatore himself behind her, when he delegated the dirty work. He had plenty of hired muscle to do these kinds of things for him.

Like kidnapping her. Or flat out killing her. Feeling helpless, she thought of how upset her brothers would be to lose her. And for a moment, Logan Quail's broad grin, as he tipped the brim of his cowboy hat, flashed into her mind. He wouldn't be at all happy if she died here tonight. Especially since he'd gone out of his way to help her escape Salvatore six months ago.

Angela gave Kate one last helpless glance before turning and running back in the direction from where she'd come. Kate tried to slow down her breathing, assessing her escape options, which admittedly looked grim. If she ran, she had no doubt the gunman would follow through on his threat of shooting her in the back.

Obviously, she'd been a fool to believe her former roommate had really been in trouble. Angie knew what her uncle was, and went to work for him at the restaurant anyway. Convincing Kate to join her, no less. Kate foolishly had taken the job, only to find out the place was run by the mafia. She'd been so glad Logan had helped her get out of there. Yet all for naught, considering she was being held at gunpoint.

Swallowing a lump of fear, she briefly closed her eyes and prayed. *Please keep me safe, Lord!*

Feeling calmer, she lifted her hands up higher in the air as a gesture of surrender, as she addressed the gunman. "Tell me what you want. Money? Information? I'm sure we can come to some sort of understanding."

"I don't want anything, but Salvatore wants *you.*"

Oh, boy. She didn't like the sound of that. Why would Salvatore want her now after all this time? She didn't know what Salvatore wanted, but there was a slim chance of surviving this if she could keep the gunman talking long enough. If Garrett had figured out she hadn't listened to his advice, maybe, just maybe, he'd send a police cruiser to the park to help her. "I'm surprised to hear that since he's the one who fired me. Does this mean he'll give me my waitress job back? I could use the money, the tips were great."

The tip of the gun jabbed the area between her shoulder blades, making her suck in a harsh breath. "Don't play dumb. Turn around and walk to the back of the building."

Never go to a second location. The knowledge reverberated in her mind, but what choice did she have? With the gun prodding her, she walked slowly, twisting her neck in an attempt to get a glimpse of the gunman. But when the gun barrel dug painfully through her T-shirt into her skin, she gave up.

She would stall as long as possible so she could remain at her last-known location.

"I'm not playing dumb. I don't know what's going on. Mr. Salvatore fired me because I was so nervous I dropped dirty dishes into his lap. Surely he hasn't held a grudge all this time? I mean, is killing me over dirty dishes really worth it?"

As they reached the back of the building, the gun barrel pressed even harder, making her bend forward at the waist in an attempt to ease the pressure. "Down on your knees," he said in a harsh tone.

No! Was he really going to kill her right here in the park? She'd thought Salvatore wanted her alive, but maybe he only wanted her dead. She sank to her knees, closed her eyes and silently recited the Lord's Prayer.

"Well, now, who's this little filly?" The familiar Texan drawl made her eyelids snap open.

Logan?

"What are you doing here, Tex? This isn't your business."

"Seems I just made it my business. She's a pretty little thing. I'm willing to pay for her. Name your price." His exaggerated Southern drawl took on a hard edge.

If she hadn't been 95 percent sure the man offering to pay for her was FBI agent Logan Quail, she'd take the bullet instead. She had to force herself to breathe as the seconds stretched into a full minute.

"I'd let you have her if I could, but Salvatore wants her alive," the gunman said. "He has a few questions for her."

"Oh, yeah? That's funny, 'cause it looks like you're about to shoot her in the back," Logan pointed out casually, as if he could care less about her fate. "Why not let me have a little fun with her first? Salvatore won't care as long as I bring her back unharmed."

"Why are you here, anyway?" the gunman demanded. "Are you following me, Tex?"

Terrified, she caught her breath as a tense silence stretched out between them. "No!" she abruptly shouted. "Don't sell me to the stranger, please. I'll talk to Salvatore. I'll tell him whatever he wants to know."

Her attempt to cause a diversion may have worked because suddenly she heard a scuffle and the pressure of the gun against her back disappeared. She caught herself before her face hit the dirt. She twisted around, scrambling backward in a crablike crawl in time to watch Logan wrestle away the gun from Salvatore's thug. Logan hit him with enough force to send the shorter, heavier guy sprawling to the ground. One more fist to the jaw and he slumped, unconscious. Logan grabbed the thug's gun before turning to her.

"Come on, let's get out of here," Logan commanded, yanking her to her feet and dragging her away from the injured gunman.

As she followed Logan, she thanked the Lord for sending him to rescue her, yet also vowed to protect her heart from being bruised by him once again.

Logan ground together his teeth with frustration, knowing he'd blown his cover in order to rescue little miss cop-wannabe, Kate Townsend, from Salvatore's hired gun Russo. Nine months of work, and hundreds of thousands of dollars, down the drain.

What was wrong with the woman? Six months ago he'd done his best to convince her to relocate somewhere far away from Salvatore, but she'd refused. She insisted on finishing her degree at the University of Chicago and it had taken all his willpower to stop from throwing her over his shoulder, physically carrying her far away and dumping her in a safe house himself.

But in the end, he'd let her go, knowing he had a job of his own to do. As part of the FBI task force focusing their efforts on eliminating organized crime, he'd had a key role to play. It had taken a long time, too long for his taste, but he'd finally gotten close to Salvatore. Had managed to earn the man's trust.

Until now.

Once Salvatore found out he'd rescued Kate from Russo, his cover would be useless. You would think she'd have enough brains to stay far away from Bernardo Salvatore, but no, here she was, trying once again to get herself killed.

"Where are we going?" she asked, as he ruthlessly dragged her through the trees and shrubs lining the back side of the park, to the road.

His jaw hurt from clenching his teeth so hard. He unclamped them and mentally counted to ten, even as he kept a wary eye out for any of Salvatore's men.

"You're hurting me," she hissed in a low voice, and he immediately loosened his grip on her wrist.

He led the way down the street and around the corner. "In here," he said, indicating the large black truck he'd parked on one of the side streets a few blocks from Stanton Park.

She climbed up into the passenger side, and he slammed the door shut behind her before getting in beside her.

"Where are we going?" she asked as he pulled out onto the street.

Since he wasn't sure, he didn't answer. The hotel where he was registered under his alias, Tex Ryan, a rancher and rich oil magnate who'd expressed an interest in investing some money into Salvatore's new horse-racing business, was too close to Salvatore's restaurant for comfort. But now that his cover was blown, he needed to get his stuff out of there, ASAP. Especially the high-tech surveillance device he'd been using to spy on Salvatore. He'd been forced to hide the disk in his suite earlier this morning, when Bernardo had made a surprise visit. The technology was top secret and he didn't dare let it fall into Salvatore's hands.

He should have kept it with him at all times, but he also couldn't guarantee he wouldn't be searched by one of Salvatore's goons. Hiding it in his room had seemed like the best idea at the time.

"Thanks for rescuing me," Kate said softly, breaking into his thoughts.

"What on earth were you doing there with Russo?" he demanded harshly.

"Russo?"

"Salvatore's thug."

She was quiet for a moment. "Angela called claiming Salvatore was trying to kill her." Kate rubbed her arms, as if she were cold. As angry as he was, he still reached over to crank up the heat for her. "But she set me up, instead."

"Why?"

Kate shook her head, helplessly. "I don't know. You must have more information than I do. How did you manage to find me?"

"I was following Russo." He scowled, not happy about this new twist. What had gone wrong? Why did Salvatore suddenly want to question Kate now? She would have been easy enough to find over the past six months.

His gut knotted in warning at the abrupt turn of events. He'd been so deep undercover that he didn't know what was going on back at the FBI headquarters, which made him feel as if he was completely in the dark right now.

Pushing the speed limit as much as he dared, he headed for the concrete driveway leading down to the hotel's underground parking garage. He parked in the farthest corner, not too far from the exit ramp, yet away from the main walkways. He got out of the truck, and Kate followed, close on his heels.

"Why are we here? Is this where you're staying?" she asked, as they wove a path between the parked cars.

"I was, but as of this moment, Tex Ryan is checking out." His boss, Kenneth Simmons, would be furious when he heard how Logan blew his cover, but what else could he do? Stand there and let Russo take her away at gunpoint? Or shoot her in the back? Just seeing her on her knees before Russo was enough to make his blood boil. For a brief moment, he'd thought he'd convinced Russo to hand her over. But then Russo had questioned his motives for following him. Thankfully, Kate had chosen that instant to beg for mercy, which had provided enough of a distraction that he'd been able to get the jump on Russo.

As they rode the elevator up to the penthouse

suite, Kate remained thankfully silent. His instincts were screaming at him to hurry. "Pack up the laptop for me," he directed. "And make sure you get all the USB drives, too."

For once, Kate did as she was told. He went into the master bedroom and retrieved the disk from where he'd taped it beneath the lamp. Once he had the disk, he tossed his clothing, including his cowboy hat and his shaving kit, into the large suitcase. Better to take everything at this point. Within minutes he was rolling the suitcase into the living room.

"Ready," Kate said, throwing the strap of his laptop case over her shoulder. As usual, she was dressed casually in a long-sleeved T-shirt and jeans, which now sported grass stains on both knees from her near miss behind the recreational center. The reminder of how close he came to losing her made him angry all over again.

"Give it to me," he said, taking the case from her. She looked so tiny and fragile with her slim build and long, honey-blond hair that he had to remind himself Kate was tougher than she looked. But no matter how strong she thought she was, he absolutely refused to let her carry his bags. "Let's get out of here."

She narrowed her gaze, clearly annoyed with him, as they rode back down the elevator to the parking garage. When the elevator doors opened, he held her back for a minute, scanning the area for any sign of Russo. He had hit Russo hard enough to keep him out for a while, but he wasn't taking any chances.

"Stay behind me," he commanded in a low voice. Astonishingly she actually fell back a step, so that she was mostly covered by his larger frame.

They'd only gone a few yards when he suddenly spied Russo walking through the rows of cars to their left. "Get down," he whispered, yanking Kate behind the cover of a midnight-blue minivan.

Kate's eyes were wide with fear, but to her credit she didn't make a sound. He pulled out the gun he'd taken from Russo, the one with the silencer, and tried to assess their options.

Russo was either planning to trap him up in the hotel suite or wait down here to ambush him by the elevator. There was also the possibility that Salvatore's men had staked out his truck, but with all the vehicles parked in the underground garage, he had to believe his truck wouldn't be that easy to find, especially since he'd made sure to stay away from the main aisles and walkways.

Had Russo called for reinforcements? Were Salvatore's men already covering the lobby and the exits?

Adrenaline surged and he knew they didn't have time to waste. He peered through the rows of cars until he saw Russo. The guy was heading toward the elevator. It was now or never.

He moved as silently as possible and stashed the suitcase under a car. Keeping only the laptop and of course the disk, he threaded his way through the rows of cars, zigzagging away from the elevator. Kate stayed right at his side, moving quietly. He couldn't let himself think about how they might be trapped down here.

The flash of headlights, followed by the sound of a car engine, filled the parking garage. He pushed Kate down behind a silver Camry, away from the beam of its headlight.

Did the vehicle belong to Russo's backup? Or another hotel guest?

He didn't dare believe the latter. Fearing the worst, he waited a moment and then picked up the pace. Speed was nearly as important as stealth. When they reached the truck, he opened the driver's-side door, the sound extraordinarily loud. He urged her to get in and then climbed in after her.

"Maybe we should wait here for a bit?" Kate suggested in a hoarse whisper.

"We can't. We'll have to risk it. Buckle up." He understood her concern, but there wasn't another option. They absolutely needed to get out of the parking garage.

He tucked the gun in his lap and took a deep

breath. The moment he started up the engine, he'd give away their position.

With a twist of his wrist, he cranked the key and the engine roared to life. He threw the truck in reverse and backed out as fast as he dared. In less than ten seconds, he shifted gears and surged toward the ramp leading to the exit.

Shouts penetrated the air and screeching tires echoed through the garage.

Russo and his men were coming after them.

TWO

"Keep your head down," he shouted. A car hurtled toward them from a perpendicular row. Another car clipped his back end, but the smaller vehicles were no match against his oversized truck. He floored the accelerator, the truck surging forward, eating up the distance between them and the exit.

Just when he thought they'd made it, the back window of his truck shattered. "Stay down," he shouted. He hunched over the steering wheel. He hadn't heard gunfire, so Russo must have gotten his hands on another weapon with a silencer.

He ignored the bullets peppering his truck as he took a sharp curve, scraping his side mirror against the wall. They finally reached street level.

He blew through a stop sign, veering directly into the stream of traffic. Several drivers leaned on their horns and swerved out of his way.

He ignored them and kept going, switching directions often and keeping a close eye on his rearview mirror in case he picked up a tail. He headed north toward the Wisconsin border, hoping that Russo would expect him to head south toward his home state.

Twenty minutes later, when he finally left the city limits, he relaxed his deathlike grip on the steering wheel. He glanced over to where Kate was sitting low in her seat, wedged in the corner between the bucket seat and the door.

"Are we safe now?" she asked, straightening enough in her seat to glance through the back window.

He slowly shook his head as he dragged his gaze back to the road. As much as he wanted to reassure her, he refused to lie. "You know better than that. We're not going to be safe until both Salvatore and Russo are locked up behind bars."

Or until the mafia boss and his right-hand man were dead.

Logan didn't dare contact his superior or anyone else within the downtown Chicago FBI headquarters, although he knew he wouldn't be able to put off the confrontation for long. Right now, he and Kate needed a place to stay, at least until he could come up with a plan.

He ran his fingers through his hair, already missing his cowboy hat. In Texas, a guy was expected to wear a cowboy hat, but not so much in

Chicago. Now that he'd been forced to ditch his Tex Ryan persona, he needed to blend in as much as possible.

Which meant he needed to get rid of the cowboy boots, too. Not to mention the big black pickup truck riddled with bullet holes. Especially since he knew there was a good chance Russo had already put out a trace on his license plate number.

All because Kate couldn't stay away from Salvatore. She knew, better than most, how the mafia boss was dangerous, but did that fact keep her away? Obviously not. Just the thought of the way she'd put herself in danger made him simmer with fury.

"Why don't you start at the beginning?" he asked, trying to remain calm as he took the next exit off the interstate, intending to hide among the anonymity of suburban Chicago. There were a string of hotels not far from the large amusement park and he hoped they could find somewhere to stay that they wouldn't be noticed. "How do you know that Angela set you up on purpose? Maybe Russo followed her?"

"Nope. She called my name seconds before I felt the gun at my back. And then she said something like, 'What are you doing? You promised not to hurt her.'"

Logan didn't even want to think about how close

he'd come to losing Kate. A fact that didn't do anything to soothe his temper. "And then what happened?"

Kate let out an audible sigh. "He told her to go back to the restaurant. I couldn't believe it when she simply turned and ran away."

"You believed she was really in danger?" he asked, unable to hide his skepticism.

She winced and nodded.

He let out a heavy sigh. "Why would she do something like this now? It's been six months since the night Salvatore fired you. There was plenty of time for them to come after you if they suspected you were feeding us information."

Kate hunched her shoulders defensively. "I don't know. She sounded scared and upset. What was I supposed to do, ignore her? I couldn't. Not when I know how her uncle gets rid of people who cross him." She paused and he kept quiet, sensing there was far more to this story than she was telling him. Finally she added, "And I thought she'd be willing to talk, to tell us what she knows about Salvatore."

Bingo. This was exactly what he'd suspected. Nothing was ever simple with Kate Townsend. "You've been investigating your father's death." It wasn't a question.

Her lips thinned but she didn't deny the allegation. Mentally he counted to ten, again, seeking patience. He'd told her to stay out of it. He'd thanked her for the information and had specifically instructed her to leave it alone.

But she'd ignored him. And now, months of work had been blown to smithereens.

She had no idea the cost. Not just in dollars. But to him, personally. Jennifer, his fiancée, had died as the result of a drug bust that had gone bad. The source of the drugs had been traced to Salvatore. It was the biggest reason he'd agreed to join the FBI task force. But now, Kate had ruined his chance to avenge his fiancée's death.

And he wasn't sure he'd be able to forgive her for that.

Kate could feel Logan's anger radiating through the confines of the truck. Deep down, she knew she deserved some of his anger, but how was she supposed to know she couldn't trust Angela? It wasn't as if she'd stayed in contact with her former roommate.

Although maybe that was exactly why she should have gone in better prepared. Why hadn't she listened to her brother's advice?

Her phone vibrated in her pocket. She reached for it, but Logan's hand shot out to prevent her from answering the call.

"It's probably my brother," she said. "He's a cop

and I told him how Angela wanted to meet with me. He'll be worried if I don't answer."

"No calls," Logan said tersely. "Especially not to your family."

Her jaw dropped open in shock. "I have to, Logan. He didn't want me to meet with Angela, and I need to let him know I'm okay."

Logan's grip didn't relax around her wrist. "But you're not okay. Salvatore wants you. He sent his thug Russo after you. Do you really want to drag your brothers into this mess?"

No, she didn't, not if her brothers would be in danger. Except she'd already called Garrett. Worry curled in the center of her gut. "How about if I just send him a quick text message?" she pleaded.

Logan finally released her. "Fine. But then shut off your phone. We can't risk someone tracking you through it. I'll buy you a new one."

Her fingers were trembling, as she quickly texted her brother.

Don't worry, I'm safe. Don't trust Angela, she tried to set me up. I'll call soon.

She sent the message and then powered down the phone.

"I thought I told you that I'd follow up on the information you gave me about Dean Ravden," Logan said.

She couldn't bear to meet his gaze. "You did," she acknowledged. She didn't add the part where she'd sensed he was annoyed with her for contacting him at all. Which was why she'd called Garrett earlier this evening instead.

Logan pulled up in front of a chain motel and threw the truck in park, turning in his seat to face her. "Yet you couldn't leave it alone, could you? My cover has been blown. Do you have any idea the significance of that? Thanks to you, thousands of dollars and months of hard work have been flushed down the drain."

His accusation lashed over her skin like a whip. "I already apologized, Logan. What do you want me to say? Maybe it was naive of me to believe Angela was really in trouble, but I couldn't take the chance that hers would be the next body found floating in Lake Michigan. I couldn't bear to have her death on my conscience."

Logan let out a heavy sigh and scrubbed his hands over his face. She felt awful about what happened, but rehashing the past wasn't going to help them now. They needed to move forward.

"Okay, wait here. I'll get two connecting motel rooms."

She didn't say anything as he slammed out of the truck. She huddled in the corner of the passenger seat, wrestling with guilt. Even though she hadn't done it on purpose, he had every right to be angry.

She closed her eyes, tears pricking her eyelids as she thought about her father. Her mother had died during her senior year of high school, and her father had been a rock of support during that difficult time. Especially for her, the baby of the family. Her brothers were already out on their own, and for a couple years it was just her and her dad. She couldn't believe he was gone.

Dear Lord, please keep my father's soul safe in Your care.

When Logan returned, she sat up and brushed away the evidence of her tears. There was nothing she could do to change the recent events, despite how much she desperately wanted to. Maybe she shouldn't have told her father what little she knew about Bernardo Salvatore. She glanced through her window as Logan drove around to the back of the building.

The hour was late, and she shivered in the cool night air as they headed inside. Logan handed her one key and used the second key for the door to his room.

"Ten minutes," he said gruffly, before disappearing inside.

A spark of annoyance pushed away her grief. She'd grown up in a household of domineering males, and didn't appreciate his tone. Obviously he wanted to talk, but she'd open her side of the connecting doors when she was good and ready and not one second earlier.

Since she didn't have any luggage, it didn't take her long to get settled. She splashed water on her face and ran her fingers through her tangled hair. Since waiting longer than the ten minutes he gave her seemed juvenile, she went ahead and strode over to unlock her side of the door.

Logan was leaning against the door frame, waiting for her. "Okay, I need to know exactly what happened with your father," he said.

"I already told you most of it," she said, crossing her arms over her chest defensively. "Dad was scheduled to appear in court to testify against a guy named Dean Ravden. He'd pulled Ravden over on a routine traffic violation and busted him for driving under the influence."

"Your dad told you this?" he interrupted.

"Yes, we talked about his cases sometimes and we had dinner together the night before. The name didn't ring a bell with me, not at first. It was only after dad's car was T-boned at the intersection that I caught a glimpse of Ravden on the news. As I told you over the phone, I recognized him as one of the men Salvatore met with at the restaurant."

"How can you be so sure?" Logan asked, his tone full of doubt. "That was a long time ago."

She narrowed her gaze and thrust out her chin. "I'm sure. I recognized his long greasy blond hair, his scruffy sideburns, his thin lips and the tiny scar buried under his left eyebrow."

"Okay, so you recognized him. What did you do then? Who did you talk to besides me?"

She tried to think back to that dark time. "I talked to my oldest brother, Garrett, first. He didn't believe me, said that the mafia wouldn't bother to make it look like a car crash."

Logan's expression tightened. "Maybe, maybe not," he muttered. "They would if it suited their purpose."

She was ridiculously pleased that he'd agreed with her, believed in her when Garrett hadn't. "Garrett may have mentioned my theory to our brothers, too. But the only other person I spoke with was my dad's boss, Lieutenant Daniel O'Sabin."

Logan frowned. "Daniel O'Sabin and Garrett Townsend. What are the names of your other brothers?"

She scowled at him. "My brothers aren't a part of this."

"Look, Kate, for all we know one of your brothers trusted the wrong person. The Chicago P.D. is known to have ties to the mob."

She didn't want to think about how some men would do anything, even sell out their brothers in blue, for a quick buck. But she knew Logan was right. "In order, oldest to youngest, Garrett is first, then Ian and then Sloan. My dad's name was

Burke, if you want to verify anything on his accident report. And I only mentioned my suspicions to my brother. When I talked to O'Sabin, I asked if he was sure the crash was an accident. I begged him to do a thorough investigation just in case it wasn't. He said he would, but then told me later that they'd closed the case as an accidental death."

Logan nodded slowly. "If he's dirty, that request alone may have been enough to make him suspicious."

"I didn't mention Ravden," she pressed, wanting Logan to understand she'd been cautious. "He couldn't know that I recognized Ravden from the restaurant."

"And you only saw Ravden on the news? Not in person?"

"Only on the news. And really, they flashed his mug shot on the screen for less than ten seconds. The only reason they had him on camera at all was because my father died on his way to testify against him."

"A fact that makes it even less likely that the mob was behind your father's accident," Logan drawled. "Why draw attention to Ravden if they didn't have to? A DUI isn't that big of a deal. Salvatore's lawyer surely would have gotten him off without a problem."

She suddenly shivered despite the warmth radiating from the heater. "Because of the cash," she whispered. She swallowed hard and dragged her gaze up to meet Logan's. "My father told me Ravden had a lot of cash on him. Enough to make him wonder if he was into drug dealing or some other illegal activity."

For a moment they stared at each other in silence. Then Logan pushed away from the door frame. "Stay here and get some rest. I'll be back in a while."

She tensed. "Where are you going?"

"I have to ditch the truck and get another set of wheels." His expression was grim as he turned away. "Keep your door locked and don't let anyone in except for me."

"Okay." She moved back and started to close the connecting door between their rooms.

"Kate?" he called.

She stopped and peered around the edge of the door. "What?"

"Don't use your cell phone, okay? Don't call or text your brothers until I pick up new phones."

"I understand," she said before closing the door with a soft click.

For a moment she closed her eyes and leaned against the door, hoping and praying that she hadn't already put her brothers, especially Garrett, in danger. She was tempted to text him again, asking him not to say anything to Ian or Sloan, but she'd promised Logan. So she kept her phone off and prayed, instead.

Please, Lord, keep my family safe from harm!

Logan headed out to the truck, and quickly slid into the front seat. He needed to get far away from the hotel before he dumped it, but he also needed to get new transportation.

Thankfully, he had a backup vehicle stashed not far from here, outfitted with traveling cash, a change or two of clothes, including his running gear and shoes. He could share the sweatshirt and sweatpants with Kate. Even the FBI didn't know about the car he'd hidden in the event of a crisis.

And this was about as big of a crisis as he'd faced since going undercover as Tex Ryan. Not that there hadn't been plenty of close calls.

Logan battled a wave of helpless fury at the way he'd been forced to abandon his cover. Yet how could he blame Kate for going to rescue Angela when he'd basically done the same thing by rescuing her? Very simply, he couldn't.

He sighed and thought through everything Kate had told him. While he didn't think it was likely her brothers were involved, he made a mental note to do some checking up on them once he returned to the motel. And then there was her father's boss, Lieutenant O'Sabin. O'Sabin might not be dirty, either, but it was likely he'd reported Kate's request up the chain of command.

And he knew only too well how high corruption could reach. To the chief of police and even state senators. In his experience no one was immune. The lure of greed and power was strong.

When he passed a well-known box store that was still open, he pulled in and quickly purchased two new disposable phones, and basic toiletries to replace what was in his left-behind luggage. From there, he drove several hours before ditching his truck in the parking lot of a large outdoor mall. He hoped the truck would go unnoticed for a while, but if Salvatore had cops working for him, they'd no doubt find it sooner than he'd like.

There was no choice but to head back on foot. He'd walked about a mile before a semitruck driver pulled over and offered him a ride. Logan gratefully climbed in, and let the older guy talk his ear off as the truck ate up the miles.

Several hours later, he drove his replacement car up to the motel and dragged himself inside. He was exhausted, but forced himself to plug in and activate the phones before booting up his computer. Refusing to feel guilty, he did a quick search on all three of Kate's brothers.

Nothing popped out at him, but he'd only done a cursory review. He'd need to do more, but right now he was so exhausted, he was swaying in his seat.

As he shut down the computer, headlights flashed against the curtained window of the motel room.

He tensed, his previous exhaustion vanishing with the sudden surge of adrenaline. Was someone out there, looking for the bullet-ridden truck? He rose silently to his feet, reaching to douse the lamp, plunging the room in darkness. Moving slowly, he crossed to the window overlooking the parking lot. He didn't move the curtains, but peered through the slim crack to see what was going on.

A basic black car, much like the type Salvatore preferred, glided slowly through the parking lot. His heart thudded painfully against his ribs. Was he overreacting? Was the driver of the black car just looking for a parking spot close to their room?

He held his breath as the auto swung in a wide curve and then headed back out to the main road.

The knot in his stomach tightened painfully and he quickly moved away from the window. He didn't believe for one moment the driver was a guest at the motel.

Logan jammed the computer in its case and then walked to the connecting doors. He opened his side and was relieved that Kate had left her side unlocked. He called her name softly as he pushed it open. "Kate? Wake up!"

In the dim light he saw her bolt upright in bed. "What is it? What's wrong?"

"We need to get out of here. Now."

She scrambled out of the bed, thankfully fully dressed, except for her shoes, which she quickly donned without bothering to untie the laces. "What happened?"

"A black car swept through the parking lot. I'm pretty sure the driver is one of Salvatore's men, looking for us." He was glad he'd gotten rid of the truck, but now realized they should have moved to a different motel, too. The one saving grace was that they wouldn't have a way to track his replacement vehicle. "We need to leave, before they return."

"I'm ready," Kate whispered, coming over to stand beside him, so close he could feel the warmth of her arm against his.

It struck him that for the first time in months, he wasn't alone. There was someone to work with. Someone to bounce ideas off. Having Kate with him was both a blessing and a curse.

He couldn't fail her. Not the way he'd failed Jennifer. He refused to let Salvatore take another person from him.

Grimly, he took Kate's arm and swept a glance over the parking lot to make sure there weren't any of Salvatore's goons around before he hustled her out to his car, a nondescript sedan with blackened windows for added privacy.

As he climbed into the driver's seat beside her, he silently vowed to do whatever it took to protect Kate.

No matter what cost.

THREE

Kate shivered when the cold night air washed over her skin, but she didn't say anything when Logan pushed her toward a dark gray four-door. The car didn't seem to have the same power as the big black truck, but if Salvatore didn't know about it, they'd obviously be far safer inside this vehicle.

She was grateful when Logan reached over to crank up the heat. He kept his gaze on their surroundings, so she did the same, looking for anything or anyone that seemed out of place. Thankfully, she didn't see anything suspicious.

Logan went in the opposite direction from the highway, taking several back roads to get away from the area. She waited until they'd ridden for several minutes before she relaxed her vigilance.

"How did they find us?" she asked. "I mean out of all the motels in all the suburbs outside Chicago, how did they look for us there so quickly?"

His mouth tightened into a grim line. "The best I can figure, they either tracked us by tapping into the GPS of your cell phone, since you didn't turn it off right away, or they had some sort of tracking device on my truck." He didn't look happy about either option.

"I'm sorry," she whispered, thinking of everything she'd done wrong since she'd received that first call from Angela. She wished she'd listened to her brother. "It must have been my phone," she said softly. "They trusted you up until tonight, right?"

He lifted his shoulder in a half shrug. "About as much as they trusted anyone, which isn't saying much. But even if it was your phone they tracked, there's nothing to worry about now. I've ditched the truck, and as long as you keep your phone off, they can't track it. Besides, I should have switched motels right after I ditched the truck."

With a spurt of frustration, she retrieved her old cell phone, opened her window and tossed it out into a farm field. Getting rid of the thing only made her feel marginally better. Truthfully, she was surprised Logan had let her off the hook so easily, considering she'd been nothing but trouble from the moment they'd met. "Where to now?" she asked, peering through the darkness.

He let out a heavy sigh. "Good question. At present we just need another place to stay. But sooner or later I'm going to have to call my boss, to let him know…" He trailed off but she knew what he'd left unsaid.

She shivered again, and not because of the cold. She couldn't imagine how angry Logan's boss would be when he discovered Logan had blown his cover and maybe risked that of the task force at large.

For her. To save her life.

She wished there was something she could do to make it up to him. But she had more questions than answers at this point. Even if she could prove that Ravden was one of Salvatore's thugs, she'd need more to link her father's death to the mob.

"Do you think we could stop at my place to pick up some stuff?" she asked hesitantly, knowing the answer because all police procedure would agree on this point. However...

But Logan was already shaking his head. "That's the first place they'd look for you."

"They might have already been to my apartment, but that doesn't mean they're staked out waiting for me," she argued gently. "I should have brought a jacket," she muttered half under her breath.

She could feel Logan's gaze rake over her. "We'll get you some stuff tomorrow."

It wasn't just warm clothing she wanted. After her dad had died, she'd been going through his things at the house, and there were family photos that she wanted. "Logan, my dad kept notes at home."

"Notes? What kind of notes? You mean about his cases?"

She winced at his incredulous tone. "Yes, but they're in a safe, way down in the basement. I found them when I went through some of his legal papers after he died."

"Any recent cases?" Logan asked.

"I didn't go through everything, but I didn't get the impression much of what he had was recent. Except I did find a newspaper clipping that I thought was odd."

"About what?"

"Remember last year, when the gaming commissioner died of a heart attack? For some reason my dad saved the article in his safe."

"John Nelson," Logan mused. "I shouldn't tell you this, but the FBI didn't think Nelson's death was an accident. Especially when the new gaming commissioner was named. William Sheppard didn't waste any time throwing his support behind the new racino bill."

"Racino?" She wrinkled her nose at the unfamiliar term. "What's that?"

"A combination of a racetrack and casino." He glanced at her. "The state of Illinois doesn't allow gambling casinos in general, not like the state of Nevada does. But this new bill granted special privileges for owners of racetracks to allow slot machines and other casino games."

"Do you think my dad might have been looking into John Nelson's death?" she asked.

"I doubt it," Logan said bluntly. "I mean, he wasn't a homicide detective, was he? What reason would he have to be investigating anything related to Nelson's death?"

"No, he wasn't a detective." Her dad had prided himself on being a beat cop, on his role of protecting the general public from danger. He'd enjoyed his work for the most part, but now she wished she'd spent more time looking over the old case files that he'd had in his safe. Much like Logan, she'd brushed them off as unimportant, since there was nothing recent. The most recent item was the clipping, and that was a year old.

Except now, she couldn't get the possibility out of her mind. What if she'd been wrong about that, too? What if those random events that had happened in the past, information her dad had kept, were in fact linked to the present?

To Salvatore and his illegal activities?

Maybe it was too late to go tonight, but somehow she needed to convince Logan to take her back to her father's house so they could get his notes out of the safe.

They couldn't afford to ignore any possibility, no matter how remote, of bringing down Salvatore's organization.

Logan found a motel just over the Indiana border and secured two more connecting rooms, thinking that it was a good thing Tex Ryan had been known for flashing a lot of cash.

Money his boss wouldn't be too happy to discover was used to hide Kate from Salvatore, instead of furthering his cover.

He made a mental note of the amount he'd have to pay back to the FBI. They both needed to get some sleep, but after a few hours, he got up and went back on the computer, searching for the article that Kate's father had kept related to John Nelson's untimely death.

He reviewed the story again, and as before, nothing jumped out at him. His boss had been convinced that Nelson's death was part of Salvatore's plan, but Nelson did have a history of heart disease. And he knew the autopsy report had been clean, so it wasn't as if Salvatore had drugged or poisoned him.

After he saved the article on his hard drive, he then went searching for information on Kate's father. The image of Burke Townsend bloomed on the screen, and he had to admit that Kate's father was an imposing figure in his full dress blues.

"What are you doing?" Kate asked.

He swiveled in his seat to look at her, upset with himself for not hearing Kate come through their connecting doors. "You have your father's hazel-green eyes," he said.

For a moment he thought she'd burst into tears.

But then she pulled herself together and came closer, her gaze riveted on his laptop computer screen. "Irish mud," she murmured. "My dad used to call them Irish-mud eyes."

They were beautiful to him, but he refrained from stating that fact. "There's a quote from the witness in the newspaper article."

She nodded. "The oncoming green truck sped up in an effort to get through the yellow light, but the small red car just drove ahead as if the driver didn't see him," she quoted, almost verbatim.

"But you still think it's suspicious?" he asked. He wouldn't put it past the mob to stage a car crash, but considering the witness statement, he couldn't ignore the niggle of doubt that crept in.

"For one thing, the driver of the green truck apparently walked away from the crash unscathed. And I've tried to find the guy except I keep hitting dead ends. The name and address seem to be fake. I couldn't validate either one. The guy does have a police record now. The system shows he has a speeding ticket and reckless driving ticket pending. But what good is that when the name and address appear to be bogus?"

"You're right. I think we should look into that a bit more," he admitted. He could use FBI resources to track down the guy. Or prove that he was using a fake identity.

"And they didn't name the witness," Kate said,

dropping down into the chair across from him. "Not even in the police report. Don't you think that's odd? Why withhold the witness's name? Especially when they used the witness statement as a reason to call Dad's death an accident?"

She had another valid point. "No good reason that I can tell," he admitted. "Officially the name should be there."

"Name and address," Kate added with a dark frown. "I can't help feeling that the document was faked. That someone made it up and then purposefully withheld the guy's identity so no one could verify whether or not the statement was truthful."

It was a potential angle to consider. "I can't think of a legitimate reason to withhold the identity of the witness," he mused. "And surely there was more than one?"

"Unfortunately, Chicago is a lot like New York. People don't always stick around to help out when something happens. Everyone just keeps going on their merry way."

He'd noticed that, too. Very different from where he grew up in South Texas. There everyone knew everyone else's business and not one person would have left the scene of an accident. Unless, of course, that person had something to hide.

"Logan, couldn't we please go to my father's house? I really want to look through the notes he left in his safe."

He suppressed a sigh. "You know it's not likely his old case notes have any bearing on Salvatore, right? It's a huge risk for very little payoff."

She scowled, her eyes dark with anger. "It is really that big of a risk? I spent lots of time at his house over the past few weeks since his death. It's not like Salvatore sent his men there to get me. They drew me out through Angela."

"All the more reason going there would be nothing more than a fool's errand." When her face fell, he felt himself caving. "Okay, fine. We'll take a look. But not until we get something to eat."

She gazed at him with relief. "Thanks, Logan. I know you're just humoring me, but I'm still grateful."

He powered down his computer and shut the lid. He wasn't sure why he'd agreed to go back to Chicago, to her father's house, except that he was fairly certain he was looking for any excuse to avoid talking to his boss.

A strategy that was working out quite well for the moment, but wasn't something he could do for much longer.

They stopped at a secondhand shop along the way to buy Kate at least one change of clothes, then ate at a truck-stop diner not far from the motel where they'd stayed. Kate wasn't surprised when Logan had checked them out of the motel. They'd have to pick someplace else to stay for the upcoming night.

"Eat a lot," he advised as he scanned the menu. "We won't be stopping again for a while."

Seeing as they served extra-large portions, judging from the plates nearby, she approved of his strategy. After the waitress brought their order, she leaned forward, capturing Logan's gaze. "I have an idea."

He lifted his eyebrows, never pausing as he dug into his Paul Bunyan–sized meal. "Yeah?"

She licked suddenly dry lips. "What if we contact Angela? Wait a minute, just hear me out first, okay?" she quickly added when he frowned at her. "I know she lured me to Russo, but she also mentioned how he'd promised not to hurt me. I think that if I talk to her, I can convince her to come with us. To turn in her uncle."

He took his time, apparently savoring his hotcakes before responding. "She also left you alone with an armed man," he said. "And you told me that she knew about her uncle long before she started working at the restaurant. Before she convinced you to hire on there."

"You're right, all that is true. But maybe she was being naive, too? Maybe she had some sort of glossed-over idea of what her uncle was really involved in? She looked shocked to see Russo holding a gun on me. Maybe if she knew the truth—"

"Assuming she doesn't already know the truth," he interrupted with the barest hint of sarcasm. "You need to know, the women in the mafia are just as ruthless, if not more so, than the men."

She didn't doubt that he knew more than she did about it, but he hadn't been there when Angela had witnessed Russo holding her at gunpoint. Her former roommate had been truly shocked. "I was there, Logan. Angela isn't cold or ruthless. I honestly believe she's in over her head."

"Let's focus on one thing at a time. First, we'll get your father's notes out of his safe. Then we'll decide where to go from there."

She dropped the issue, hoping he'd at least consider her idea. Maybe they couldn't totally trust Angie, but could they turn her against her uncle? She wanted to believe they could.

When they were finished eating, Logan paid the bill at the cash register before leading the way out to the car. She was a little surprised he took the interstate to Chicago. "I take it this car isn't registered in your name?"

"You're right, it's not." He seemed preoccupied by his thoughts, and she hoped he wasn't thinking of ways to get rid of her. She'd had trouble sleeping last night, worried that he'd force her to go into a safe house. "Don't worry, this car can't be traced back to me."

She hadn't really thought it could. "Is it okay to

call my brother again?" she asked, pulling out her new, disposable cell phone.

He grimaced, but then slowly nodded. "I guess, but whatever you do, don't tell any of your brothers where you are or that you're with me."

She rolled her eyes as she opened the phone and turned it on. "I'm not stupid, Logan. I just don't want them to worry."

"I never said you were stupid," he muttered. "But right now, you can't trust anyone. Not even your family. Your brothers wouldn't betray you on purpose, but they could accidently say something to a cop who's secretly working for Salvatore."

"I know. I hear you." She wasn't about to do anything to put her family in additional danger. She took a deep breath and dialed her eldest brother's number. Garrett answered the phone before it even rang.

"Hello?" he answered warily.

"Garrett, it's me. Kate." She was surprised he'd even picked up since he wouldn't have recognized the phone number.

"Katie? Where are you! We've been worried sick!"

"Didn't you get my text message?" she asked, taken aback by another uncharacteristic emotional outburst. Garrett had always been the calm, stable brother. He'd been married, but his wife had left him a few years ago. He'd grown even quieter after his divorce, holding himself aloof from the rest of the family. "I told you I was fine."

"You didn't answer your phone and now you're calling me from some unknown number. What's going on, Katie? You need to get home ASAP."

"Look, I only called to let you know that I'm fine. You're not going to hear from me for a while, okay? Tell Ian and Sloan not to worry."

"Katie, come home," Garrett pleaded. "Between the three of us, we'll keep you safe."

Her throat welled with emotion, and she wanted nothing more than to be with her family. But Logan was right. Salvatore was after her. She couldn't bear for her family to be dragged into this mess. "My staying away is the best way to keep the three of you safe. I promise I'm fine. I'll check in as often as I can, okay? But don't call me. Wait for me to contact you."

Garrett sputtered, obviously unhappy with her response, but she cut him off. "I love you, Garrett. I love all of you. I'll talk to you later, okay?" She quickly hung up the phone and then powered it down.

Logan glanced over at her. "Are you all right?" he asked.

She forced herself to smile. "I'm fine. They're just a bit protective, which is nothing new."

Logan nodded again, and fell silent. She was relieved to have some time to pull herself together.

Talking to her brother had shaken her more than she cared to admit.

They made good time on the way back to Chicago, and within an hour and a half, they were back inside the city limits. "You'll need to give me directions to your father's house," he said.

She pointed out turns and soon they were in the familiar neighborhood where she and her brothers had grown up. They hadn't had a lot of money, but there had always been an abundance of faith and love.

"There, the small white house with the black shutters, house number 824."

"I see it." Despite his words, Logan drove right past it, taking a left at the next intersection.

She bit back a cry. "Where are you going?"

"We need to make sure the house isn't being watched," Logan said, as he made another turn, as if heading back toward her father's place.

She batted down a flash of impatience. "I think if Salvatore was going to make a move on my father's house, he would have done it four weeks ago, right after his death."

"Kate, he's still searching for you," Logan said.

She let out a breath, knowing he was right. Did Salvatore have enough manpower to waste time staking out her apartment and her father's house? She doubted it, but kept her eyes peeled for anything that might seem out of place. She caught sight of an elderly woman walking a small white dog. "That's Mrs. Gordon and her dog, Mac. They live two houses down from my dad."

Logan drove around the block again, going a different way this time. And then he surprised her by pulling over to the curb. "We're going to walk from here."

She knew he meant through the backyards, as her father's house was located directly behind the green-and-white house.

They climbed from the car. She made sure she had her key in hand as they quickly darted under the old apple tree, using it as cover on their way through the yard.

Just as they reached the edge of her father's property line, a loud explosion rocked the earth. She cried out as she was thrown backward, into Logan. She hit the ground hard and could only stare in shock as her father's house went up in flames.

FOUR

"Are you all right?" Logan hissed in her ear. She barely managed to nod before he hauled her up to her feet. "Let's go."

She tried to dig in her heels, wanting to resist as Logan dragged her back the way they came. "Wait, we have to check," she protested. She wanted to see what she could salvage from her father's house before the fire took everything.

"No way. We have to get out of here before one of the nosy neighbors sees us."

She had little choice but to follow him to the car, the scene from the explosion replaying over and over through her mind in excruciating slow motion. The faint wail of sirens could be heard, slowly growing louder. Numb from shock, she barely managed to buckle her seat belt as Logan stomped on the gas pedal, heading out of the neighborhood where she'd spent her early years.

"I don't understand," she whispered, trying to

gather her scattered thoughts. "Why would someone blow up my dad's house?"

Logan didn't answer right away, and when she
glanced over at him, she could see the tense angle
of his jaw, his eyes glued to the road. After several long moments, he finally responded. "Good
question. Who else knew what your father had in
the basement?"

She shook her head, unable to believe that Salvatore would have blown up her father's house over
a few notes. "Other than me and my brothers? No
one."

"Not his boss, Daniel O'Sabin?" Logan pressed.
"Are you absolutely sure?"

She closed her eyes and rubbed her throbbing
temples. No, she wasn't sure. She wasn't sure about
anything anymore. "I don't think so. There's no
reason for my dad to confide in his boss. But it
doesn't matter, because no sane person would blow
up a house because of a few notes. Why not send
someone in to steal them? Wouldn't that make more
sense?"

"You mentioned he had a safe," Logan said with
a frown. "Is it possible that someone planted dynamite beneath the safe? The explosion knocked us
off balance but we weren't seriously hurt. Could
be that the source of the explosion was down in
the basement."

"Maybe." She was forced to agree, even though

she still thought Logan's theory was a stretch. "But the safe isn't that big. Salvatore could have had his guys steal it in order to take it someplace else to crack it open."

The farther they got from her dad's house, the more Logan relaxed. She could hear him draw in a deep breath and let it out slowly. Was he remembering a similar explosion from six months ago? This was the second time they'd managed to escape by the skin of their teeth.

Thank You, Lord! Thank You for sparing us!

"Maybe the dynamite served a dual purpose," he murmured. "First to get rid of whatever evidence your father might have saved and second to scare you."

She shivered, staring sightlessly out the window as Logan headed to some new location. She didn't like to admit that he might be right.

She hated the thought that Salvatore was constantly one step ahead of them. Almost as if he knew what they were going to do before they did it. And despite the faith she had in Logan and in God, she couldn't fight the sense of overwhelming despair.

Logan kept shooting glances at Kate, sensing she was far more upset than she'd let on. And he couldn't blame her, not when everything in her father's house—photographs, other personal items—were all likely gone forever.

He knew they shouldn't have gone back there, although he never once considered that their lives would be in danger from an explosion. No, at the most, he'd figured they'd need to dodge a few of Salvatore's men.

Even though Logan had provided a logical explanation to Kate about why her father's house had been blown up, he had trouble believing it himself. Granted, he knew better than most that Salvatore was unpredictable, but at the same time, it seemed like overkill to draw such attention to Kate's father's house, when Salvatore had gone to great lengths to make Burke's death look like an accident.

None of it made any sense. Unless the explosion wasn't a warning for Kate at all, but for Logan?

A warning for both of them, most likely, as Salvatore probably figured out they were working together against him. And Logan felt slightly sick knowing that Salvatore had endless resources to keep coming after them.

When the orange fuel light went on, he pulled into a small corner gas station. As he filled the tank, he tried to come up with another plan of action. He was well overdue to call his boss, but he didn't want to do that, yet. Not until he had something more on Salvatore.

He needed to be able to redeem himself. And he needed desperately to find a way to bring Salvatore to justice.

After he paid in cash for the gas, he climbed back into the driver's seat. When he started the engine, Kate put her hand on his arm as if to stop him. "Wait. We need to head back to Chicago, to try and find the guy who hit my father."

The warmth of her hand surprisingly helped him relax. "Kate, you were right, okay?" he said gently, turning partially in his seat to face her. "I believe you. I believe Salvatore sent one of his goons to kill your father. But trying to find the driver has already proven to be a dead end. If he used a fake name and address, we won't find him."

"So what are we going to do?" she asked, her Irish-mud eyes wide and fierce. "How can we prove it?"

And wasn't that the million-dollar question? "Maybe we need to focus on Dean Ravden."

Her eyes widened and then gleamed with anticipation. "Yes, that might work. Maybe we should get a copy of the original police report my father filed?"

"You read my mind," he drawled. "And we can use my laptop to research him, as well."

She let her hand drop from his arm, and he found he missed the warmth of her touch. Which was ridiculous because he wasn't interested in anything that resembled a relationship. Not now, not ever. Now with anyone, but especially not with Kate.

Kate was too young. Too stubborn. And too intent on becoming a cop.

Three strikes and you're out.

He didn't say much as he headed once again toward downtown Chicago. They would have to request a copy of the police report, and he knew they wouldn't just hand it over right away, since the cops loved to tie everything up in red tape.

When they arrived at the small precinct where Burke Townsend had worked as a beat cop, he reached over to stop Kate from getting out. "I need you to stay here."

Immediately, her eyes narrowed. "What for? You can't think we're in danger at a police station?"

He strove for patience. "Look, normally they make you wait up to five days for a copy. I'm going to flash my FBI badge to get it right away."

Comprehension dawned in her green eyes, but her scowl only deepened. "So I can't come with you because I don't have a badge?"

"Exactly." He left the car running, just in case. "Stay here. Hopefully I won't be long."

She folded her arms over her chest and gave a terse nod. He walked inside, not at all convinced his badge was going to help him. Although he needn't have worried since the gum-chewing, bubble-blowing young woman behind the counter was more than impressed and almost fell over her feet to get him a duplicate of the report.

"Thank you, ma'am," he drawled, laying the Texas accent on a little thicker than normal as he folded the report. "Much obliged."

"Oh, no problem," she gushed. "If you need anything else, don't hesitate to ask."

He gave her a nod, missing his cowboy hat and boots more than ever as he left the police station. He refrained from rolling his eyes when he saw that Kate had climbed into the driver's seat.

"Did you get it?" she asked eagerly.

He nodded. "Move over, I'm driving."

"Chauvinist," she muttered before awkwardly scooting over the console and back into the passenger seat.

"It's my car," he pointed out, tossing the folded police report into her lap. "Besides, you have to read through that, since you know your father better than I do. Let me know if anything jumps out at you."

She fell silent, scanning the pages as he pulled away from the curb and turned into traffic. He headed toward Indiana, to find another innocuous motel to stay the night, preferably one with internet access.

Kate sucked in a harsh breath, causing him to glance over. "What is it? What's wrong?"

"This doesn't make sense," she murmured, half under her breath.

"What?" he demanded. "What doesn't make sense?"

"The timing. My dad normally worked day shift. After all, he had thirty years in and they always fill shifts by seniority. Everyone wants day shift."

"Yeah, that makes sense."

"But this police report states that my dad pulled Dean Ravden over at 0422. Almost three hours before the normal start time of his shift."

He didn't think that was any big deal. "Obviously he switched shifts with someone."

Kate was shaking her head. "No, I don't think so. Why would he? The rookies work graveyard and he wouldn't agree to switch, staying up all night without a really good reason. Certainly not just to do some rookie a favor."

Maybe she had a point. "So then why would your dad be out on the streets in a squad car in the wee hours of the morning?"

"There's only one reason that makes any sense," she said slowly. "I think my dad must have been following Ravden."

The more Kate thought about the possibility, the more she grew convinced she was on the right track. It was the only thing that made sense, and she was irritated with herself for not figuring it out sooner.

Her dad had led her to believe he was on his regular shift when he'd told her that he'd pulled Ravden over on a suspicion of a DUI.

"What possible reason would he have to follow Ravden?" Logan asked in a tone that made her believe he was more than a little skeptical. "You recognized him because you saw the guy talking to Salvatore at the restaurant, right? After your father had already given him a ticket. There's no way your father could have known Ravden was working for Salvatore before then."

Logan's words resonated in her head, making her stomach clench with dread. "He could have known, if he was watching Salvatore," she said, forcing the words from a throat tight with guilt.

There was a long, heavy pause. "You actually told him your suspicions about Salvatore?" he asked in disbelief.

Yes, she had. Tears stung her eyes, and she blinked them back with an effort. What was wrong with her? She deserved Logan's disgust and anger. Logically, she knew she probably shouldn't have mentioned Salvatore to her father. But she'd wanted her dad to be careful, as his beat included Salvatore's restaurant. Had wanted him to know the truth so that he didn't stumble into something dangerous. She'd known that Salvatore had cops on his payroll and had wanted her father to be aware of the potential danger.

Instead she'd caused his death. She buried her face in her hands and rocked back and forth, trying not to drown beneath the tsunami wave of guilt and sorrow.

"Kate, don't. Come on, it's not your fault."

But it was. She knew it was. Even Logan knew it was, or he wouldn't be trying so hard to comfort her.

"Kate, please. I can't stand to see you like this."

His hand was on her shoulder, but she couldn't bring herself to look at him. She sensed the car wasn't moving. He must have pulled over to the side of the road.

Her fault. Her father's death was ultimately her fault. And somehow she hadn't even realized it until now.

She felt Logan gathering her into his arms, no easy feat with the console between the bucket seats. For a moment she allowed herself to lean against him as she tried to pull herself together.

He smelled wonderful. His aftershave mixed with his unique musky scent managed to soothe her raw nerves. For a moment she wanted more than anything to be the type of woman Logan might be attracted to. Someone beautiful and glamorous, who hadn't spent her entire life wanting to be a cop.

But she wasn't that woman. And Logan wasn't the man for her. For one thing, he'd already bruised her heart. And besides, he was a cop, too. She'd tried dating a cop, Sean Parker, one of her brothers' friends, and that had been a total disaster. She knew she needed to find a guy with faith, someone who would support her dreams rather than trying to change her into something she wasn't.

Taking a deep breath, she let it out slowly. Then silently begged for forgiveness.

I'm sorry, Lord. I'm so sorry. Please forgive me!

"Kate, please don't do this. You haven't done anything to feel guilty about."

She realized she must have spoken out loud. Somehow, she found the strength to lift her head and face him. "Yes, I do. For telling my father about Bernardo Salvatore. For believing Angela was in danger. For blowing your cover." Her voice was husky from crying and she sniffled loudly, desperately wishing for a tissue. "I've done nothing but make mistakes."

"Here." Logan pressed a packet of tissues into her hand. As she blew her nose, he smoothed damp strands of hair from where they were stuck to her cheek. "You didn't make mistakes, Kate. I'm sure you told your father about Salvatore in order to warn him, right? And you believed Angela, mostly because you didn't want her death on your conscience. And you didn't try to get captured by Russo. Salvatore obviously must have targeted you because you were poking into the truth around your father's death. One of the cops working for him must have tipped him off. So don't you see? Salvatore is running scared, from you."

A ghost of a smile tugged at the corner of her mouth at the thought of big, bad Salvatore running from little ole her. But Logan had a point. Salvatore had reacted in a big way, to her quest for truth.

She looked up at Logan at the same time he'd lowered his head toward her and for a long, heart-stopping moment she thought he was about to kiss her.

But then he eased back, and the brief moment of opportunity vanished. Which was good, because she couldn't afford to allow herself to get side-tracked.

"Wait here, I'll get us two connecting rooms." Logan quickly opened the driver's-side door and hopped out, striding toward the main office of the Motel 6 he'd obviously found while she was wallowing in her misery.

She used a few more tissues while she waited, trying to repair the damage she'd done. She pulled down the sun visor to peer in the mirror, grimacing at the red blotches on her face, which matched her lovely red nose.

"Pathetic," she told herself as she flipped up the visor. She needed to be strong if she was going to find the proof she needed to lock Salvatore up for good.

The evil man deserved no less than life in prison. And she vowed to do whatever was necessary to help put him there.

Logan was relieved that Kate looked better when he returned with two motel room keys. He climbed in beside her and tossed her one. "We're in rooms eleven and twelve, on the other side of the building."

"Great." Her smile didn't reach her eyes, but he wasn't going to complain since watching her fall apart had unnerved him badly enough. Kate was always so strong, so stubborn, that watching her dissolve, her shoulders shaking with sobs, had wrenched his heart.

And then he'd almost messed up everything by kissing her.

He was anxious to get settled into their respective rooms; he could use some distance.

She disappeared into room twelve, while he let himself into room eleven. Even though he hadn't unlocked the connecting door between their rooms, he thought he could still smell the distinct scent of vanilla that followed her everywhere.

He scrubbed his hands along his face, the overnight growth of his beard starting to itch. They still had the few supplies he'd picked up at the store before they went on the run, so he dug for the razor.

He felt more human after he shaved. It was too early to eat dinner and too late to eat lunch, so he booted up his computer to start a search on Ravden.

After ten minutes of not hearing any sound from Kate's room, he set aside the computer and went to the connecting door. He unlocked and opened his side, then lightly tapped on hers.

"Just a minute," she said and he heard her footsteps as she approached the door. When she opened it up, he was relieved that she wasn't crying again. "What's up?"

"Aah, nothing, really. I just wanted to make sure you were okay." *Lame, Quail, really lame.* "I didn't hear anything. I thought you might be sleeping."

"So you decided to wake me up?" she asked and he found himself smiling at her tart tone. "I was reading the Bible, which is obviously just as quiet as sleeping."

Now he really felt like a fool, because he'd forgotten that Kate was a Christian. Not that he was an atheist or anything; he just didn't display his religion, or lack thereof, for everyone to see. "I thought we'd eat dinner around six if that's okay with you?"

She cocked her head and leaned on the door frame. "Changing the subject, Logan?"

No, he wasn't changing the subject. He was

avoiding it. "Get some rest," he advised. "I'll let you know if I find anything."

She straightened and her gaze zeroed in on his computer. "I forgot about your laptop," she said, pushing her way past him to enter his room. "Are you searching for Dean Ravden? Have you found anything yet?"

"Yes and no," he said with a sigh, as he followed her toward the small table where he'd been working. "Look, I just told you that I'll let you know if I find anything. Two people and one laptop won't work."

"I'll just sit and watch you work." He wanted to groan when she plopped into the chair next to his. "I won't disturb you."

She was already disturbing him, but he didn't let on as he returned to his seat. He'd started with the FBI computer program, but hadn't found anything on Ravden. He thought it was too early to get data about her father's house explosion, but he went to the local media webpage anyway. The explosion had made headline news, and he clicked on a live camera link where a reporter stood in front of Burke Townsend's house.

"We're here live, outside a quiet neighborhood still reeling from the shock of an explosion at the house belonging to former police officer Burke Townsend. As you know, Burke Townsend died several weeks ago, on his way to testify in court on an alleged DUI case. As you can see, there is a lot of activity going on behind us between the police and the firefighters, and we have confirmed reports of a person being inside the home when the explosion hit."

"What?" Kate whispered in shock. She leaned forward as if she could see past the news reporter. "I have to call my brothers."

Logan hadn't thought of her brothers, and nodded as she fumbled with the phone. But when the news reporter continued, he put a hand on her arm to stop her.

"The police have not confirmed the identity of the body at this point. However we have a source claiming the deceased is Dean Ravden, the suspect that Officer Townsend was planning to testify against in court."

"I can't believe it," Kate said, dropping her phone in her lap. "Do you really think that's true? That Ravden was actually inside my dad's house when it blew up?"

"I think that it's entirely possible that Salvatore used the explosion to get rid of Ravden," he said slowly and with grim certainty.

And he knew this was just another message from Salvatore, letting them know he was playing for keeps.

FIVE

Kate dialed her disposable cell phone with shaking fingers. She desperately needed to talk to her brothers, to make sure they were okay. To make absolutely certain none of them had been inside their father's house.

Logan was still searching for information on Ravden, although if the guy was really dead, then there wasn't much point. It wasn't as if Ravden could lead them to Salvatore now.

"Kate?" Garrett answered on the first ring. "Are you all right? Where are you?" he demanded.

"I'm fine." She winced, knowing she should have called earlier, right after the explosion. No doubt her brothers had been worried. "Have you spoken to Ian and Sloan? Are they both okay?"

"Thank You, Lord," Garrett whispered. "Katie, you have no idea how worried we've been." Her brother sounded truly rattled, as if he was hanging on the end of his rope.

She knew how protective they were and didn't

plan to tell any of her brothers how close she'd been to their dad's house when it exploded. "What about Ian and Sloan? I need to know they're okay, too."

"They're fine—trust me. I've spoken to both of them. They want to call you, Katie, and talk to you themselves. They want to know you're all right. And they want you to come home."

Home. For a moment tears threatened but she ruthlessly shoved aside the remorse. She'd always considered her father's house *home,* but now it was gone. There was nothing left but charred walls, smoke and ashes. "You'll need to convince them I'm fine, Garrett. I already told you, I won't put any of you in danger. Look, I have to go but I promise I'll be in touch."

"Katie, wait," Garrett said, but she snapped shut her phone and powered it off. Disposable phones were harder to trace than personal cell phones, but not impossible. Who knew what sorts of resources Salvatore had at his fingertips? She knew Logan expected her to keep it off except for emergencies.

"Are you all right?" he asked.

"Yeah." She forced a smile, even though the previous peace she'd found by reading the Bible had vanished after the horror of the newscast. "I was worried one of them might have been at my father's house, but they're all fine."

"I know." He put his arm around her shoulders and gave her a gentle hug.

She savored his embrace for a moment, before reluctantly pulling away. She knew from her criminal justice classes that getting an accurate ID on a dead person took time. And if the body was burned, fingerprints weren't going to help. They'd need dental records or other DNA evidence. All of which took lots and lots of time. "How do you think they managed to ID the body as Ravden so fast?"

"I suspect they found some sort of ID that was planted at the scene," Logan said slowly. "And I also think some dirty cop let the information leak on purpose."

She didn't like the thought of a corrupt policeman, but she knew he was probably right. "Salvatore is still trying to scare me, huh?" she asked, striving for a light tone.

"Yes, he is." Logan's tone was blunt.

Okay, then. No sugarcoating that one. She squared her shoulders. "Then we have to be smarter than he is," she said with conviction. "And find a way to keep him on the defensive."

Logan nodded, although she knew that was all easier said than done. "You mentioned you couldn't find the driver of the green truck that barreled through the intersection, hitting your dad. Let's see if we have better luck using the FBI resources at our disposal," Logan said.

She nodded, and Logan motioned to the police report that he'd handed her earlier. At least the trip to the police station hadn't been a total bust. She still couldn't believe Dean Ravden was dead.

Once again, she wished she could convince Logan to call Angela. If she could talk to Angie, maybe she could convince her to turn on her uncle. And even if her former roommate didn't know anything that would really help them, at the least she would like to have Angie safely away from harm.

She was very worried Angie's body would be the next one they stumbled across.

Logan glanced at his watch when his stomach grumbled loudly, not surprised to see the hour was well past six. "Let's go," he said, shoving away from the computer. "My eyes are starting to hurt from staring at the computer screen anyway."

Kate nodded, but didn't say anything as they grabbed their stuff to leave. She'd been unusually quiet over the past hour or so.

"I thought we'd eat at the steak house that's located just down the road a ways," he said, with a quick check outside before holding the door for her to move past him. "If you don't mind steak?"

She lifted a shoulder. "Steak is fine."

He scowled, longing for the return of her feisty attitude because, even though she'd often driven him crazy, he preferred that attitude over this new subdued passiveness. Once they were both settled in the car and on the highway, he asked, "What's your favorite food?"

Finally, she smiled. "Italian, but I don't mind steak, either." There was a pause before she suddenly asked, "Are you really from Texas?"

He glanced at her in surprise as he pulled into the parking lot of the restaurant. "Yes, why do you ask?"

"Just curious." She fell silent again as they got out of the car and walked inside. Thankfully, there were plenty of available seats for a Thursday night.

They were seated in a booth near the back, and Logan sat so that he was facing the door. "I figured you could tell just from my accent. In fact, my parents still live on the ranch where I grew up." Everything in his real life had helped in creating his cover as Tex Ryan.

Her smile dimmed and he mentally kicked himself for bringing up his parents, now that hers were both gone. "That's nice," she murmured, staring down at the menu.

Time to change the subject. He glanced at his menu, although it didn't take long for him to figure out what he wanted to have. "The T-bone sounds good."

"I doubt they have Texas-sized portions," she teased, as she closed her menu. "I'm having the New York strip."

The waitress returned to take their order. He was surprised when Kate ordered her steak medium rare. "Brave woman," he said. "You know it will be red on the inside, don't you?"

"I learned to eat medium-rare steaks from my dad. He used to say, 'Walk it slowly through a warm room.'" The fleeting smile on her face made his chest hurt.

"Sounds like you miss him," he said.

She gave a little sigh. "More than you could possibly know." She was quiet for a moment and then pulled herself together. "Enough wallowing in the past. Tell me, what do your parents think of your career? I'm surprised you didn't want to take over the ranch, keeping it in the family."

Normally, he didn't like talking about himself, but in this case, since she was clearly missing her dad, he obliged. "My younger brother, Austin, has already pretty much taken over the ranch, the Lazy Q, and since that was what he always wanted, I figured he deserved it." He took a long gulp of his water and looked around for the waitress, hoping she'd bring refills. "Ranching is tough—long hours and backbreaking physical work."

"And your current career is so much easier?" she teased.

He didn't want to talk about his current career, especially since he wasn't even sure he still had one. Still, he responded, keeping his tone light. "Sure. Piece of cake."

"What made you want to go into law enforcement?"

"My uncle was the sheriff of our town. I knew early on that I wanted to be a cop."

"Similar story to mine, I see." Before he could argue that point, she asked, "Have you talked to your boss yet?"

"No. And I don't plan to, until I have some good news to share."

"Listen." She leaned over the table, dropping her voice low so their conversation couldn't be overheard. "I want you to reconsider talking to Angela."

He scowled, wishing she would drop it already. Why in the world was she so set on getting in touch with her roommate? "No."

Her gaze narrowed, but she refrained from saying anything more when their server brought over their meals.

He was about to dig into his meal when Kate clasped her hands together and bowed her head to pray. Feeling like an idiot, he bowed his head and waited for her to finish, before picking up his fork. He was too hungry to care that the steak wasn't exactly done as he'd ordered it. Close enough.

"God would want us to forgive her, and to help save her from Salvatore," Kate said, between bites. "And what if she has information that could help us?"

Information that would implicate them, more likely, but he didn't voice his skeptical thoughts. "I'm impressed you can forgive her so easily. And I understand you're worried she's going to end up dead, but we have no way of knowing whether or not she wants to be saved."

The way she looked at him, with something akin to pity shadowing her gaze, only made him mad. Didn't she understand how much trouble he was in already? How many rules he'd broken by bringing her along as he searched for evidence to use against Salvatore? And how many others in the task force may now be under greater scrutiny, at bigger risk?

"I guess you don't believe in God," she said as she scooped up a forkful of mashed potatoes.

"I never said that I didn't believe," he responded testily. She was going from one sore subject to another and he wished she'd just drop them both.

"Really?" She looked happy at the news. "That's wonderful."

"Not really, considering I haven't been to church since my fiancée died."

"Oh, Logan," she whispered. "I'm so sorry."

He didn't answer, keeping his attention focused on his food. And thankfully, she did the same, without asking a dozen more questions.

Questions he had no intention of answering.

* * *

Kate wanted to ask Logan more about his fiancée, but knew from the closed expression on his face that he wasn't going to satisfy her curiosity.

When they'd finished their meal, they headed back to the motel, and she found herself wishing they had two laptops so they could both search.

Watching Logan work wasn't very much fun, yet at the same time, she couldn't make herself leave.

"What do you know about Steve Gerlach?" he asked, after he booted up his computer.

"You mean other than he's the officer who responded to the scene of my dad's murder?" she asked drily. "Not much, why?"

"I've discovered that the driver of the truck that hit your dad used a fake name. The real Joseph E. Canton was sixty-seven years old and died three years ago."

"I knew it!" She was relieved to discover her instincts hadn't failed her, after all. When no one had believed her, she'd thought maybe she was losing her mind. "I knew it wasn't an accident. Too many things felt wrong."

"What we need to know is whether or not we can trust Officer Steve Gerlach," Logan said grimly. "Because either he neglected to write down the name of the witness, or someone else scrubbed it from the report."

The idea of some dirty cop going to such lengths

made her feel sick to her stomach. A cop who had turned his back on a fellow officer, no less. "I've heard my dad talk about him, which isn't that surprising since they were both on day shift. I could also ask my brothers," she offered.

"No, let's just call him, see what he says on the phone." Logan picked up his disposable cell phone and dialed the police station. "This is FBI agent Logan Quail, I need to talk to Officer Steve Gerlach, as soon as possible."

She leaned close in an attempt to hear what the dispatcher said. "He's not working this evening, I'll put you through to his voice mail."

"Do you have his cell number? Because I need to speak to him right away."

"I'm not supposed to give out personal cell numbers," the dispatcher said. "Can you provide confirmation that you're with the FBI?"

"Call my boss at the Chicago office to verify my identity if you need to," he offered. "I'll wait."

"No, that's fine. I'll give you the number." There was a brief pause and then she rattled it off. "Gerlach, 555-2920."

"Thanks, I appreciate your cooperation."

"I can't believe she did that!" Kate exclaimed. "She's not supposed to give out those numbers and she couldn't know for sure you weren't bluffing."

"Actually, I kind of was," he said.

"Wait," she said, as he typed in the number. "I

think I should call him. For one thing, I'm a cop's daughter and I think I can use my brothers as leverage if needed. If he hears you're a Fed, he'll clam up."

Logan reluctantly handed her the phone. She took it and pushed the button to make the call. She half expected it to go to voice mail, but he picked up on the third ring, his voice deeply masculine. "Hello?"

"Officer Gerlach, my name is Kate Townsend and my father was Burke Townsend. You probably also know my brothers, Garrett, Ian and Sloan. I'm sorry to bother you but I have a quick question about my dad's accident report."

"Oh, yeah? I knew your dad, he was a good cop. What kind of question?"

At least he hadn't hung up on her. "You didn't write down the name of the witness."

"That's not a question and besides, you're wrong. I did write down the name. I clearly remember taking her name and her address."

The witness was a woman? She glanced up at Logan, gauging his reaction. "Do you remember her name?"

"Something common, like Jones or Smith. Her first name ended in a *Y,* like Sally or Mary. I don't remember the details. It was like a month ago, although maybe it will come to me."

"Tell him we want to meet, tonight if possible," he whispered.

"Officer Gerlach, would you be willing to meet me tonight? You can pick the place and the time."

She practically held her breath, hoping he wouldn't refuse. "Tonight, huh?" There was a pause. "You familiar with the Oakland Cemetery?"

"Yes, I am." She'd heard about Oakland from her brothers. it wasn't far from the fifth district cop shop and sometimes the rookies would meet there after working the graveyard shift before grabbing breakfast.

"Meet me in the southwest corner at eleven o'clock."

She thought it was odd he wanted to meet there, although the cemetery wasn't that far from the fifth district police station and maybe he felt it was safe enough. "All right. Thanks again."

"Don't thank me. I'm only doing this out of respect for your dad and your brothers," he said curtly before hanging up.

"I can't believe he agreed," Logan murmured when she handed him his phone. "Although why he would choose to meet in a cemetery is beyond me."

"I think it's a cop thing," she said, turning toward the computer screen. "We only have an hour before we need to hit the road, so let's see what else we can find."

But further searching proved fruitless. "Come

on, let's go," Logan said, pushing away from the computer. "We need to get there early, anyway."

She grabbed her sweatshirt and the police report before heading outside. As Logan navigated the dark streets of Chicago, she hoped and prayed that Officer Steve Gerlach could remember the name of the witness that somehow failed to be listed on the official police report.

Because right now, it seemed that every lead they managed to uncover only resulted in a dead end.

Logan didn't like meeting in the cemetery, but since Kate had agreed, there wasn't much choice but to go along with it. He was slightly relieved to discover it wasn't located too far from the police station, as promised. But it was pitch-black, no lights whatsoever. At least the darkness helped cover them just as it provided cover for the bad guys.

And he wanted desperately to believe that Steve Gerlach wasn't one of the bad guys.

He parked on the opposite side of the cemetery from the designated meeting spot, and made sure his weapon was loaded as they prepared to walk through the graveyard.

"Stay behind me," he murmured, as they slipped past several engraved headstones.

For once she didn't argue, but fisted her hand in the back of his dark sweatshirt. He concentrated on moving slowly and silently, avoiding the grave markers as much as possible.

He froze when he heard something, but after several long moments there was nothing but silence, so he continued toward the southwest corner of the cemetery.

They were pretty much on time when they reached the proposed meeting spot. He hunkered down behind a large crypt. "Stay here," he whispered.

Kate's fingers dug into his arm in protest, but he didn't plan to leave her there. He only wanted to peek around the corner, searching for signs of Gerlach.

His eyes had grown accustomed to the darkness, and he swept his gaze carefully over the area. But if the cop was there, he wasn't in plain view.

The center of his back itched with warning, and he tightened his grip on his gun. "See that smaller crypt over there?" he asked, keeping his mouth close to Kate's ear. When she nodded, he continued, "That's our destination, but stay low."

When she nodded a second time, he crouched down and moved as quietly as possible over to the smaller crypt. When he got there, he stumbled over something soft. Human.

"Look out," he whispered urgently, grabbing Kate's arm so she wouldn't trip over Gerlach's prone figure. And now it was clear why the cop wasn't in plain sight.

She gasped, and he leaned over to feel for a pulse, not entirely surprised to discover the officer they were supposed to meet was dead. There was a bullet hole in the center of Gerlach's forehead. Ordered by Salvatore? Or was the scene simply set up to make it look like a mafia hit?

"I can't believe he's been murdered!" Kate whispered in horror. "How did this happen? Was he followed? How could anyone know he was meeting us here?"

He pulled the officer's phone from his pocket at the same instant he heard the sound of a silencer. "Get down!" he cried, yanking on her arm just as a bullet whizzed past his head.

SIX

Logan threw Kate down on the ground and covered her body with his, protecting her as best he could. Whoever had killed Steve Gerlach was still out there, only now he and Kate had become the targets.

Thankfully, they'd managed to get behind the small crypt. But how long did they have until the gunman came looking for them? Probably not long. They had to move. Now.

"Can't breathe," Kate whispered in a hoarse voice.

He tried to shift his weight to the side, lifting his head as much as he dared in order to assess their surroundings. He couldn't see any sign of the hit man, but the cemetery provided a lot of cover.

Cover that would work both ways—hiding the killer and helping them escape.

He gauged where the shooter might have been based on where he heard the *poof*ing noise and the angle of the bullet whizzing past his ear. The shot had come from the northwest. Even if the guy was on the move, they had two options, to head farther east or farther south.

Or stay put, but he didn't like that option. Considering the shooter had already pinpointed where they were. They needed to move, the sooner the better. Their vehicle was located to the east, so that's where they needed to end up.

"You're going first. Fifty feet in front of us and slightly to the right are two large headstones. Head that way and use them for cover," he whispered in Kate's ear. "I'll be right behind you."

She hesitated, but then nodded. He moved enough so that she could get to her hands and knees, gathering herself so that her feet were beneath her. She took a calming breath and waited for him to give the signal before she sprinted from behind the crypt. He was impressed with her speed, and made sure he was directly behind her as he followed, in case the gunman fired at them.

But even after they ducked down behind the headstones, there was nothing but the sound of their ragged breathing and his heart hammering in his chest.

"Do you think he's gone?" she whispered, her eyes wide in her pale face as she braced herself against the back of the tombstone.

He shook his head. Just because the gunman hadn't fired at them, didn't mean he was gone. In fact, he could have been hiding, waiting for them to move. And if he'd done that, he might know just where they were now. What they needed was some sort of distraction.

He tightened his grip on his weapon. Before using it, he glanced around to determine their next hiding place. "See that tall crypt, about twenty feet to your right? That's our next spot," he said in a low voice.

"Okay," she agreed.

He took a deep breath, and then stood and shot in the direction from which the silencer sound had come. After he shot, the shrill sound echoing through the night, he gave Kate a nudge, and they darted out from behind the tombstones, crossing over several graves.

As they ran, he heard another *poof*ing sound seconds after they both ducked behind the tall crypt. Only once they were safe did he become aware of a sharp pain in his left arm.

Dazed, he reached up with his other hand to investigate and discovered his sleeve was damp. When he pulled away his hand, dark smears stained his fingertips.

Blood. He'd been hit by that last bullet.

Kate did her best to swallow her fear, her heart beating so fast she was becoming dizzy. Flattened against the cold concrete structure, she rested her forehead against the unyielding stone, realizing she'd have to get used to being shot at once she graduated from the police academy.

She closed her eyes for a moment, wondering how her brothers faced this every day. Was Logan right? Was she cut out to be a cop?

Dear Lord, keep us safe!

Logan was moving beside her so she lifted her head and glanced over at him. "What are you doing?" she whispered.

"I need you to tie this around my arm," he said, pulling the string free from the hood of his sweatshirt. "As close to my armpit as you can."

It took several moments for the meaning to sink into her tired brain. "You're hit?" she whispered, unable to hide her horror.

"It's not bad, but hurry. We have to keep moving."

She wasn't a nurse, had no clue how to fix a gunshot wound, but at the moment all she needed to do was to apply a makeshift tourniquet. So she took it from his hand and looped it around his bicep, tying it snugly as high as she could. "Is that too tight?" She could barely see what she was doing in the dark.

"No, it's fine."

A gunshot wound wasn't *fine,* but there wasn't time to argue. They needed to get back to the car so Logan could get to a hospital. Now that she knew he was wounded, the sense of urgency was almost unbearable.

Her mind raced. Twice now, the gunman had gotten close, too close, to hitting his target. "He must be holed up somewhere, watching us," she whispered.

In the darkness, she could see a faint smile. "Good deduction, Sherlock."

His attempt at humor, in the face of danger, and being wounded to boot, gave her a boost of badly needed confidence. "We need another diversion."

"The last one didn't work so well," he pointed out.

No, it hadn't. But she refused to give up. She scanned the area, searching for—something. Anything.

And then she saw it. A metal cross anchored on top of a small crypt, the one where they'd first taken cover. She took out her cell phone and gauged the weight in her palm.

Thanks to her older brothers and four years as captain of her high school softball team, she had a decent arm and a good eye. She could imagine how the scene might play out, the brief diversion possibly buying them enough time, if she could convince Logan to go along with her plan.

"We have to split up," she whispered.

"No way." Despite the whisper, his tone was fierce. "I'll keep covering you."

She ground her teeth in frustration. "He can't shoot both of us at the same time. Splitting up will confuse him." And maybe, just maybe, they could get far enough away that they could call the police station across the street for help. The dispatcher couldn't trace a cell phone signal like they could a landline, which meant she'd have to be able to speak loud enough for them to hear and understand what she was saying, without giving away her position to the gunman.

She prayed that the cops who responded weren't the ones on Salvatore's payroll.

"I'm going to hit that cross with my phone, and the noise will help distract him as we both head in different directions. From there, he won't be able to watch all three spots, which will help us get farther away. We'll both move every few minutes, keeping him off balance." Her plan could work, if he'd just trust her.

"Use this, instead." He pressed a decent-sized rock into her hand. "Hang on to your phone."

The rock was perfect, so she nodded. "You go east and I'll go north."

"You go east, *I'll* go north," Logan responded. East was closer to the spot where they'd left the car, and clearly Logan wasn't going to give on this one. Even though he was the wounded one.

"Fine. Get ready." She picked out her next hiding spot and then took a steadying breath. She peeked around the corner and took aim, throwing the rock on a wing and a prayer.

There was a loud clang, and they both darted off, heading in different directions. As soon as she was safely behind the protection of another tall headstone, she became acutely aware of how much she missed Logan's reassuring presence.

The darkness seemed more oppressive, more sinister without him beside her. She tried to focus on the reassuring sounds of the crickets and frogs.

She couldn't let herself think of the fact that Logan might be hit again. Or losing blood despite the tourniquet she'd placed. After waiting just thirty seconds, she moved again, this time with more stealth, as she slid on her belly over the ground to the next crypt.

A muffled noise made her freeze, but she realized the sound was probably from Logan. She darted to the next crypt, and then saw the dim glow of the streetlight.

Their car was less than fifty feet away.

She clutched her cell phone, wondering if she were far enough away from the shooter to call the police station. But after opening her phone, she realized the number was on Logan's phone, not hers. They'd used his phone to call the station, asking for Steve Gerlach's number.

There was the option of calling 9-1-1, but she

couldn't be sure that the officer sent by the dispatcher wasn't on Salvatore's payroll.

Her brother Garrett's number was in the phone, but he wasn't close enough to help. No, their best bet would be to get to Logan's car. She moved to another gravestone, and then decided to go straight for the car.

It wasn't until she was within arm's reach of the vehicle that she remembered Logan had the keys.

Logan ignored the throbbing in his arm as he moved as silently as possible from one tombstone to another. As much as he hated to admit it, Kate's plan was a good one. He hadn't heard any more *poof*ing sounds, which made him think their shooter was confused as to where they were hiding, exactly the way Kate had anticipated.

He'd gone north at first, but then angled toward the street where he'd parked the car, grimly realizing he should have given Kate the keys.

No point in berating himself. He quickened his pace, hoping to meet her there, only to trip over a dead tree branch lying between tombstones. He managed to catch himself before he fell, pain zinging up his injured arm.

He froze, plastering himself against the tombstone, hoping that the gunman hadn't heard the noise. When there was nothing but silence, he moved steadily toward the next tombstone.

The nagging itch in the center of his shoulder blades eased, and he thought it was possible the gunman had given up and left, but he didn't break from cover, unwilling to risk his life on gut instinct. So he continued moving toward the road. And when he saw Kate dashing toward the car, he couldn't help feeling a surge of relief.

Safety and freedom were just a few yards away. He grabbed the key fob from his pocket and unlocked the car, the soft beeping noise echoing loudly in the night.

Kate threw a glance over her shoulder in his direction as she opened the car door and dove inside.

He could see her sitting low in the driver's seat, the top of her head barely visible as she waited for him. The minute he reached the car, he tossed her the keys as he scrambled for the passenger seat. She fumbled for a moment before jamming the key into the ignition, turning it and stomping on the gas.

As she peeled away from the curb, he closed his eyes, partially because she was driving like a maniac, but mostly because he was so thankful they'd made it out of the cemetery alive.

And for the first time since his fiancée had died, he found himself praying. *Thank You, Lord! Thank You!*

Kate drove as fast as she dared, putting mile after mile between them and the cemetery. Imitating Logan, she turned several times, in case anyone was trying to follow them. But this late at night, there weren't too many cars on the road and it was easy to see no vehicle was tailing them.

She glanced over at Logan, more worried than she wanted to admit when she saw him sitting calmly in the passenger seat with his eyes closed. She racked her brain for the location of the closest hospital.

"Go back to the motel," he said, as if he'd read her mind.

"Logan, you need a doctor." She glanced around anxiously. Where were those little blue H signs when you needed them?

"No hospital. You know gunshot wounds have to be reported."

His eyes were open now, and she relaxed her death grip on the steering wheel. "So what? We need to report this, Logan. And we need to call the police about Steve Gerlach."

Now that they were safe, the images came flooding back. Steve Gerlach's prone body lying on the ground with the horrible dark bullet hole in the center of his forehead. How did they find him? Why did they kill him?

But of course she knew why he was dead. And it was her fault. She'd called him, asked about the witness that had described her father's car accident.

The witness whose name had been mysteriously erased from the police report.

Steve Gerlach had been killed so she couldn't prove the entire so-called accident that had claimed her father's life was nothing more than an elaborate setup to hide the truth.

The truth about her father's murder being linked to Bernardo Salvatore.

"Kate, turn left up at this next intersection," Logan said, breaking into her thoughts.

She turned, and then realized they weren't that far from the motel. She glanced at him to find that he was loosening the string she'd tied around his arm. "What are you doing?"

"I need to assess the damage," he said calmly, as he somehow maneuvered his left arm out from the sleeve of his sweatshirt.

The T-shirt he wore beneath the sweatshirt was short sleeved, giving her a far-too-vivid view of the angry red gash on his arm. She quickly averted her gaze, gluing her eyes to the road. "How bad is it?" she asked, almost afraid to hear the answer.

"Not nearly as bad as I feared," he said. "Not deep enough to have hit an artery or vein, so the tourniquet was overkill. The bullet tore through some muscle, that's all."

Tore through some muscle? "Sounds painful," she murmured, fighting to keep her tone steady. Cops were expected to stay cool under pressure, right? And while she wasn't a nurse, she knew basic first aid. She should be able to handle this.

Not that a bullet wound qualified as first aid in her mind, but she had to admit he was right about going to the hospital. Who knew if the cops who came to investigate would be on Salvatore's payroll? Maybe if she could arrange for one of her brothers to investigate? But no, they'd have to call the district where the incident occurred.

Incident. As if being hunted through a cemetery in the dead of night by a mafia gunman was nothing more than an incident.

"Kate? Are you all right?" Logan asked.

"Yes. Fine. Why?"

"Because you just passed the motel."

"Oh." She scowled, because he was right. She pulled into the next driveway and made a U-turn. This time, she managed to pull into the motel, driving around the building and parking in the spot in front of their connecting rooms.

She turned off the car, feeling an overwhelming sense of exhaustion. But she couldn't afford to cave under the pressure. There was still too much to do.

Gathering every ounce of strength and willpower she possessed, she handed Logan the keys and slid out from behind the steering wheel. By the time she came around to the other side, Logan had opened his motel room door and held it for her with his good arm.

She ducked inside, and then waited as he closed and locked the door behind him. He plopped down on the chair closest to the door, as if he were as weary as she was.

Sending him a tired smile, she grabbed the yellow plastic ice bucket. "Stay there, I'll get some hot water and towels."

Without waiting for a response, she disappeared into the small bathroom, gathering everything she'd need. They didn't have any bandages or gauze, though, so the washcloths would have to work until the stores opened in the morning.

She returned with her arms full, to see Logan sitting with his head leaned against the wall, eyes closed and legs stretched out in front of him. He looked so peaceful. The blood trickling down his arm was the only indication of the day's violence.

When she set down the bucket, water sloshed over the side. "Are you ready?" she asked, even though he looked as comfortable as she was nervous.

"Yes. Have at it, Nurse Nancy."

There he went again with the lame jokes. She flashed an eye roll before taking one of the hand towels and dipping it in the hot water and using it to clean the wound.

He flinched, but didn't protest. She tried to work quickly, making sure the entire area was clean before she used the washcloth as a bandage and then wound a larger towel around it to keep the smaller cloth in place.

"All finished," she murmured. She took the bucket of red-stained water and the bloody towels back to the bathroom.

When she returned, she almost smacked right into Logan, as he was standing just outside the bathroom door. He caught her shoulder with his right hand and then hugged her. "Thank you, Kate," he whispered against her hair.

She closed her eyes and leaned against him for several long moments, sinking into the embrace, even though she knew he only meant to offer comfort. And friendship.

"You're welcome," she whispered against his T-shirt. His chest was strong, yet supple, the beat of his heart beneath her ear reassuring. She could have stayed like that for the rest of the night, and despite her desire to protect her heart from being hurt again, she found herself lingering in his arms.

But this wasn't the time to relax, reveling in the fact that they were alive and safe. There was still work to be done. She reluctantly stepped away, intending to remind him that they had to call the police about finding Officer Gerlach, when Logan caught her off guard by tipping up her chin and lowering his mouth to hers in a heart-stopping kiss.

SEVEN

Kate couldn't help succumbing to Logan's kiss, even though she knew it wasn't smart. Logan was going to walk away from her once this was over, the same way he had six months ago.

But she didn't possess the strength to pull away from him. Instead she moved into the kiss, enjoying the way he hugged her tightly, exploring her mouth with his.

When he finally lifted his head, she gasped for air and leaned against him, her knees week. All too soon, he eased her away. Glancing up at him, she saw regret reflected in his eyes.

"I shouldn't have done that," he said in a low, husky voice.

Knowing that he regretted the kiss they'd shared only made her mad. Dropping her arms but not moving, she said, "Thanks, that makes me feel so much better."

He winced at her caustic tone. But what did he

expect? She'd enjoyed his kiss, even though it was clear he didn't feel the same way.

And she needed to accept he never would. Which was just fine with her. She didn't need another domineering male in her life. She wanted someone who would partner with her, not try to control her. Was it too much to be accepted for who she was? Seemed all the men in her life wanted to change her into something else.

But this wasn't the time to worry about her personal life. Or lack thereof. She waved her hand. "Never mind about that, we have to call the police and tell them about Gerlach," she said, changing the subject. "And about being shot at in the cemetery."

"Look, I'll call in an anonymous tip about Gerlach, but as far as going in to give statements about what happened tonight? No way." Logan's expression was grim. "Especially not after hearing how Gerlach's accident report was tampered with. Salvatore doesn't have the ability to change a police report. But a cop working for Salvatore from inside does."

He was right, but that didn't mean she had to like it. The very thought of dirty cops on Salvatore's payroll made her sick to her stomach. "I could call my brothers. They could help investigate."

"Kate, do you really want to drag them into this?

Gerlach is dead because he talked to us. Or because someone knew he was going to talk to us."

Guilt squeezed her chest, making her light-headed. "I still can't believe he's dead. I feel so helpless," she murmured.

"Get some sleep," Logan said firmly. "I'll call one of the guys on the FBI task force to let them know about Gerlach. I'll make sure they understand the officer's death is related to Salvatore."

She nodded her agreement with his plan and eased around Logan to head to her own room. But in the doorway, she paused and turned back toward him. "Do you really think it is?" she asked. At his frown, she added, "That Gerlach's death is really linked to Salvatore?"

"Yes, I do. You were right all along, Kate. Your father's death wasn't an accident. He was killed so that he wouldn't blow the whistle on Salvatore."

She nodded and stepped over the threshold into her own room. Hearing the conviction in Logan's tone made her feel better. She wasn't in this alone anymore. Logan believed her.

She needed to believe that, together, they'd find a way to prove it.

And hoped and prayed they wouldn't die trying.

Logan did his best to ignore the pain in his arm so that he could sleep. But it wasn't easy. For one thing, he couldn't get comfortable.

And when he closed his eyes, he kept seeing the dead cop he'd stumbled over. Officer Gerlach.

Who'd killed him?

He figured that Gerlach must have called someone. Maybe the second officer who'd come to the scene of Kate's father's car crash? Or his partner?

As possibilities whirled in his mind, he must have drifted off to sleep.

"No, stay back!" he hissed, putting out his arm to stop Jennifer in her tracks, pressing her back against the building. "I'll take care of these guys."

She nodded, holding her gun at the ready, her eyes wide.

He vowed to convince Jennifer to quit the DEA once they were married. He couldn't take having her exposed to danger this way. But right now, they were on their own. They'd stumbled upon the drug deal going down, giving him no choice but to intervene. He'd called for backup, but there wasn't time to waste. These guys wouldn't be here long.

Taking a deep breath, he waited for the drugs to exchange hands before he made his move. "Stop! Police!"

The two guys sprang apart, and he followed the one with the money. But the guy with the drugs shot at him. He ducked beside the parked car and by the time he peered around the bumper, he saw the man was facing Jennifer, both of them pointing their weapons at each other.

Shoot him, *he silently urged. But Jennifer seemed frozen, unable to move. No! He brought up his weapon but too late. Jennifer crumpled to the ground. He pulled his trigger and watched the man with the drugs fall, while the guy with the money managed to get away. He rushed over to her side.*

Except that it wasn't Jennifer lying there on the ground in a pool of blood. It was Kate, her long blond hair stained red. His heart squeezed in his chest as he screamed her name. Kate! Kate!

"Logan? What is it? What's wrong?"

His heart was pounding in his chest as he forced away the remnants of the nightmare. He looked up at Kate, hoping his mind wasn't playing tricks on him again. "You're alive."

She frowned and reached up to feel his forehead, as if checking for a fever. "Yes. And so are you. You must have had a bad dream."

Yeah, that was putting it mildly. She had no idea. "I'm fine," he said in a low, husky voice. "Sorry to wake you."

She shrugged, and moved away as if uncomfortable being alone in his room in the darkness. It took everything in him not to ask her to come back. "No problem," she said lightly. "Just try to get some sleep, okay?"

"Sure. You, too." He waited until she returned to her own room before getting up to drink a glass of water. It helped, but he knew with sick certainty nothing was going to erase the image from his mind of Kate lying on the street dead.

He buried his face in his hands, trying to shake off the effects of the dream. He had to keep Kate safe. Because he wouldn't survive another innocent death on his conscience.

The next morning, Kate woke up to find the sun streaming through the motel room window. She staggered up and out of bed, amazed to realize it was almost nine o'clock in the morning.

Falling asleep after Logan's nightmare hadn't been easy. But she'd managed to get some sleep after all, and could only hope he'd been able to, as well.

She quickly showered and dressed, wrinkling her nose at having no choice but her wrinkled clothes. When she heard a loud thump from Logan's room she rushed over to open the connecting door.

"What happened?" she asked, when she found Logan braced against the wall. "Are you all right?"

"Yeah, I'm fine." He straightened and carefully made his way to the small table. "I tripped over my own two feet."

She narrowed her gaze at the way he avoided looking at her. First the nightmare last night and now this. Was his injury worse than she'd realized? She fought a sense of panic. "I need to go to the drug store to pick up some bandages and antibiotic ointment. I'll be back in a few minutes, okay?"

"Sure, I'll be here." A faint smile tipped his mouth. "Bring back some breakfast, too, okay?"

"No problem. But I'll need some cash and the car keys."

"Right." Logan dug into his back pocket and pulled out his wallet. He handed her a twenty and the keys she'd returned last night. "Stay safe."

His concern grated a bit on her nerves. She was going to the drug store, not something that could be considered dangerous by any stretch of the imagination. "I'll be back soon."

Despite being out in broad daylight, she couldn't help watching the rearview mirror like a hawk, to make sure she wasn't followed. She'd hoped to enjoy the few minutes of normalcy, but instead found herself hurrying to return to Logan. She was worried about him, and the thought of facing the danger of Salvatore alone was terrifying.

Picking out the dressings took longer than she'd anticipated. Afterward, she stopped at the first fast-food joint she saw to pick up egg sandwiches on the way back to the motel. Thankfully, no one seemed to pay her any attention.

She used her key to get into her room, and then tapped lightly on the connecting door. "Logan? Are you hungry?"

"Yeah, come in, it's open."

She wasn't sure if it was a good thing that Logan was still sitting at the small table where she'd left him. Then she relaxed when she realized his hair was damp from the shower. "Let's eat first while the egg sandwiches are still warm, then I'll look at your arm." She was glad he had another towel wrapped around the wound.

She set the bag of food on the table between them, closed her eyes and put her hands together. "Dear Lord, thank You for providing us food to eat, and please keep us safe from harm. Amen."

"Amen," Logan echoed. She glanced at him in surprise. He'd never done that before when she'd prayed. She found herself hoping that Logan had a relationship with God after all, as she dug into her meal.

They both ate in silence, and she wondered if she should have gotten two sandwiches for Logan when he devoured his in record time. "I can go out for more," she offered.

"No need, I just want to finish up here and get back on the road."

Back on the road? She frowned. "Why do we need to leave?"

"Because we can't afford to stay too long in one place," he said curtly. "I need to make sure you're safe. Check out time is eleven o'clock."

She suppressed a sigh as she finished her sand-wich. When he began unwrapping the towel from his arm, she went to fill the plastic ice bucket once again with hot water.

The injury to his bicep looked a little better, at least from what she could tell. The deep furrow was starting to scab over a bit and didn't look infected. Still, she washed it again and spread a liberal layer of antibiotic ointment over it before she lightly wrapped gauze around it, more to keep the area from being irritated than anything else.

"We should have split up earlier," she said as she finished. "Then he wouldn't have hit you."

Logan's mouth thinned. "Or maybe he would have hit you," he said harshly. "Did you think of that possibility?"

"You act as if I'm helpless," she said, struggling to understand what was driving his seemingly single-minded determination to keep her safe.

"And you're acting as if you're already a cop. But you're not. So don't try to compare yourself to me. And if I had my way, you never would be. Women shouldn't be cops."

For a moment she was shocked speechless. Logan had never spoken to her this bluntly about his views before. He was worse than her brothers! How could he be so chauvinistic?

And then she caught a glimpse of the sheer agony in his eyes, and realized there must be more going on with him than what he was saying. Was this the root of his nightmare? She strove to keep her tone light. "What was her name?"

His scowl deepened. "I don't know what you're talking about."

She wasn't put off by his attitude. "Your fiancée. I know you loved her, but now I'm thinking that she must have been someone you worked with. A partner maybe?"

He winced and turned away, and she knew she'd hit the nail on the head. She'd known he'd lost his fiancée but she hadn't realized, until right now, that she had also been a cop.

Just like Logan.

No wonder he felt the way he did.

She couldn't stop herself from reaching out to him. "Logan, you're not alone. I'm here. And don't forget, God is with you, too, if you're willing to believe and to lean on His strength."

He let out a harsh sound, something between a laugh and a groan. "That's just it. I don't believe. Otherwise, why would God take Jennifer away from me? Why didn't He take me instead?"

She ached for him and wished he'd tell her what had happened. Although did it really matter? His fiancée was dead. And he'd obviously loved her very much. "It's not up to us to question God's will, Logan. But I believe He has a reason. One that just hasn't been revealed to us yet."

He shook his head, showing his disbelief, and

pulled away, rising to his feet. "Grab your stuff from your room. We have to hit the road."

She reluctantly returned to her room to pack her meager belongings. So, Logan's dislike of her chosen career wasn't personal, but was related to Jennifer, the woman he'd loved and lost. She didn't know if that made her feel better or worse.

And she was troubled by his lack of faith. She slid into the passenger seat beside him and silently vowed that while he helped her find her father's murderer, she would do her best to help him rediscover his faith.

Logan drove to the other side of town, keeping to the less-traveled back roads and wishing he'd kept his mouth shut.

Why had he blabbed about Jennifer? Kate didn't need to know about his personal life. Besides, he'd lost Jennifer well over two years ago. He should be over it by now.

And he was over Jennifer's death. But in his dream, or rather his nightmare, Jennifer wasn't the one who'd died.

Kate was.

He gripped the steering wheel tightly as he navigated around a large tractor rambling in front of him on the long stretch of county highway. He couldn't afford to be distracted by the dream.

They had to figure out their next move.

"I think we should call Angela," Kate said, breaking the silence. "We're pretty much out of options."

"I have Gerlach's cell phone," he said, avoiding her comment about Angela. He was still angry about her former roommate setting her up in the first place. No matter what Kate said, he wasn't about to trust the woman. "I went through his call history and wrote down all the numbers."

"Why didn't you say so sooner?" she demanded. "Where's the list?"

"There's only one other number he called after we contacted him," he said, pulling a piece of paper out of his pocket and handing it over. "It's the last one on the bottom."

"I don't recognize it," she murmured, staring at the motel stationery he'd used for his notes. "But we should try calling it."

"No!" He shot out his hand to stop her. "Not yet. Not until we do a little investigating first."

She frowned, and then nodded. "Okay, I can see your point. We don't want to tip him off, do we?"

The band of fear that had tightened around his chest eased enough for him to breathe. "No, we don't. Once we get settled, I'll boot up the laptop and see what we can find. There were a few text messages there, too, but they were pretty cryptic. Nothing so obvious as a name or anything."

"Okay, I'll try to have patience. Although we

already know that it's a local number, based on the Chicago area code."

Yeah, he'd already noticed that much, too.

"'See you later,'" she murmured, reading through the text messages. "That one came in shortly before we contacted him."

"Yeah, and from a number that shows up on his call list a lot," he added. "Probably a girlfriend."

"Do you think she might know something?" Kate asked excitedly.

"I don't know." And truthfully, he was loath to find out. The last thing he needed was to drag any more innocent bystanders into this mess.

Having Kate here beside him was bad enough. Maybe he liked working with a partner more than he'd thought, but he'd rather have another FBI agent instead of a woman he was starting to care about.

A woman he'd kissed.

A woman he wanted to kiss again.

Grimly, he dragged his concentration back to the issue at hand. Hopefully, the phone numbers and text messages he'd taken from Gerlach's phone wouldn't turn out to be another dead end.

Because the sooner he brought Salvatore to justice, the sooner Kate would be safe. And he desperately needed to know that she was out of danger. Before he moved on to the next case.

EIGHT

Kate spent some time in the uncomfortable motel armchair going over the text messages, but there really wasn't much to be gleaned from them. It wasn't a surprise that Steve Gerlach had a girlfriend. Kate wanted to talk to her, to see if she knew anything important.

Although there was a strong chance she wouldn't know anything that would help them. Kate knew from her brothers and her father how a lot of cops didn't like to bring the ugly aspects of their jobs home to their families. It was only when Kate had made it clear she was pursuing the same career in law enforcement that her father had started opening up to her.

Grief stabbed deep and she momentarily closed her eyes, remembering the way her dad had looked the last time she'd seen him, with his green eyes crinkling at the corners when he smiled. The way he'd hugged her at the end of their dinner together, engulfing her in the comforting scent of his Old Spice aftershave.

She swallowed hard and took several deep breaths to get her emotions under control. She had to remind herself again that her dad, a devout Christian, was up in heaven now, finally reunited with her mother. Their pastor was right—he was in a much better place.

She swiped the moisture from her eyes, sniffled loudly and tried to focus again on the phone numbers Logan had written down. Her gaze kept lingering on the number Gerlach had called about thirty minutes before their scheduled meeting in the cemetery. Something about it was vaguely familiar.

And suddenly she figured it out. "Logan, I know this number Gerlach called right after he talked to us! It's one of the numbers in the third district police station."

"The third district?" he echoed in surprise. "Are you sure?"

"I'm sure. My brother Garrett works there. All the phones in that district have the same first three numbers. I didn't recognize it at first, because I don't call him there often. I normally use his cell phone."

"At least that will be easy enough to check out. But Gerlach worked out of the fifth district, didn't he?"

"You're right, Gerlach did," she echoed, staring

at the phone number with a deep frown. "So why would he call someone in another district? That doesn't make any sense."

"Could be that he has a friend there," Logan mused under his breath. "A friend who just happens to be dirty."

"Maybe," she agreed. All along she'd assumed that Gerlach had died because he'd talked to them, but there was another possibility. "Or maybe he was the dirty cop." She didn't want to think that of him, but it was an avenue that had to be considered. "Maybe he called someone else to let them know I was asking questions."

"Then why kill him?" Logan asked. "Why not just wait for us to get there and take us both out of the picture?"

She glanced at the makeshift bandage she'd applied to his arm. "That was part of their plan, obviously."

"But killing Gerlach before we got there doesn't make sense."

She could almost imagine how it might have gone down. "It does if Gerlach balked at killing us. Maybe he made it clear to the dirty cop that he'd meet with us and try to shake us off the trail. But the dirty cop wanted us to be silenced forever, and Gerlach wasn't keen on that approach. So the dirty cop killed him, and then waited for us to show up, and then tried to take us out."

"It's possible," Logan said slowly. "I guess at this point, anything is possible."

"So many deaths," she murmured. "I just don't understand. Is there no value to human life? How is it possible that money is more important?"

Logan glanced at her and shrugged. "Money and power, the two go hand in hand."

She knew he was right, but she simply couldn't comprehend it. Salvatore's men, even the cops he had on the payroll, had to know the mobster didn't value human life. Was the risk really worth the benefit? Were they so blind they couldn't see that they were disposable?

She rubbed her eyes and then leaned back against the seat cushion. She'd started down this path to avenge her father's death, but that wasn't the driving force any longer. Salvatore had to be stopped. Soon.

Because it was just a matter of time before he killed again.

Kate barely glanced at the name of the motel Logan had picked for their next hideout. It didn't really matter much. They'd be here for forty-eight hours at the most.

Idly, she wondered just how much cash he had left to keep getting motel rooms like this. Granted, they were staying at cheap places, but still, how long could he afford to keep throwing away money?

She couldn't shake the feeling of helplessness. It seemed that for every step forward they took on the investigation into her father's murder, they slid back three.

"I managed to get two connecting rooms again," Logan said when he'd come back out to the car. "Here's your key."

"Thanks." She took the small plastic card. "Logan, I know I've mentioned this several times already, but don't you think it's time to call Angela Giordano? It's a long shot to think we'll be able to figure out who Gerlach called at the third district. We need someone who knows Salvatore. Like Angela."

He narrowed his gaze. "You do remember how she led you to Russo, right?"

"Yes, and I clearly remember her saying something like 'you promised you wouldn't hurt her.'" She couldn't explain the deep need she had to try to save her former roommate. "Just let me call her. Please?"

He stared at her for a long moment, before giving a terse nod. "Fine, call her. But we're going to use Gerlach's phone. I don't want her to have your number."

"It's a deal." She went into her own room first and opened the windows to get rid of the musty smell. Not that she was complaining. Clearly these were the sorts of places that took cash with no questions asked.

She splashed water on her face and then headed over to open her side of the connecting door. Logan already had his ajar, so she knocked lightly before crossing the threshold.

"Here's Gerlach's cell phone," he said, handing it to her. "The battery is already half-gone so we'll need to keep it off when we're not using it since we don't have a charger."

"We might be able to buy one," she said as she punched in Angela's number. The phone rang several times before going to voice mail. "Angie, this is Kate. I want to help you stay safe. Call me back at this same number as soon as possible." She hung up and glanced over at Logan. "Can I leave it on for a few minutes?"

"Sure." He was reading something intently on the computer screen, so she moved closer to see what had snagged his attention.

"Is this the racino you mentioned?" she asked, tapping the photo on the screen. The picture of the racetrack looked like something you would see if you went to the Kentucky Derby.

"Yeah, that's it all right. The Berkshire Racetrack."

And a casino. *Racino.* "Are the slot machines inside the building?"

He nodded. "And blackjack tables." He grimaced. "Perfect way to get rid of dirty money."

"It's not right that Salvatore can get away with

it," she muttered, scowling darkly. "Is the public really so blind that they can't figure out it's partially owned by the mafia?"

He shrugged. "Who knows? Gambling is much like any other addiction. Easy enough to keep a blind eye to the parts you don't want to see."

She couldn't understand what anyone saw in gambling. Especially if you didn't have money to lose in the first place. But Logan was right. The people who spent a lot of time gambling probably couldn't care less who owned the place.

The phone in her lap vibrated and rang simultaneously, making her heart leap into her throat. She grabbed it, recognizing Angela's number. "Angie?"

"Kate, I'm so glad you're all right. How did you escape Russo?"

It was on the tip of her tongue to let Angie have it for setting her up, but that was in the past. Time to move forward. "Never mind that now, I want to make sure you're safe. You need to get away from your uncle, Angie. Before it's too late."

"I know. I'm so sorry, Kate. I didn't know…" Angie's voice trailed off.

"It's okay, Angie, we all make mistakes." Hadn't she made the biggest one of all, by mentioning Salvatore to her father in the first place? "Just get away from the restaurant. Find someplace to hide."

"I will. Actually, your brother Garrett called me. I'm going to meet him in a few hours."

"Garrett called you?" She didn't bother to hide her surprise. Logan just frowned. "That's great. He's a cop. He'll keep you safe."

"Yeah, well, he did promise that, too. But the main reason he wants to talk to me is to find out what I know about my uncle," Angie said drily. "He was not pleased with me."

"No, he wasn't at all happy that you allowed Russo to capture me," Kate murmured. Logan's snort was probably heard through the phone by Angie.

"I'm sorry, Katie. Honestly, he said he just wanted to talk to you."

Angie should have known better than to believe her uncle's thugs would simply talk to anyone. But that wasn't the point. "Do you have information on Salvatore? Because if so, I'd like to hear it, too. Where are you meeting Garrett? I'll join you."

Hearing this, Logan stood over her, shaking his head for emphasis.

"I don't know anything," Angie said in a weary tone. "You know what it's like working at Salvatore's. We see the customers who come in here, but they're pretty good at not talking in front of us. And I wish I did know more about my uncle's business associates. All I know is that he's tried to kill me."

Kate caught her breath, even though she shouldn't be shocked to hear the news. Hadn't she feared this all along? It was the main reason she'd agreed to meet Angie at the park in the first place. "What happened?"

"He sent Russo after me. But I'd already left my apartment, was just inside the stairwell when I saw him kick his way inside. I've been on the run ever since."

"Garrett will help you, don't worry," she soothed her. "I'd still like to hear from you, too."

"All right. Look, I have to go. I've been riding the subway all day, and I need to change trains. I'll talk to you later."

"Sounds good. Bye, Angie." She snapped Gerlach's phone shut and then turned it off to preserve the battery. "She's safe, at least for the moment."

"Why did your brother get in touch with her?" Logan asked.

"Probably because he's trying to help by getting information about Salvatore," she told him. She held up her hand to keep Logan from interrupting her next words. "We need to meet up with them to convince Garrett to back off." She'd warned her brother to stay out of it, but he hadn't listened. And suddenly, she was very afraid that Garrett would somehow end up just like her father.

Dead because of her.

"There's no reason for us to meet. He can fill us in on whatever he finds out. Besides, I told you all along that Angela probably doesn't know much," Logan countered.

"How do you figure? I found out quite a bit while I was waitressing at Salvatore's," she pointed out. "If you remember, that's when I called you."

How could he forget? Six months ago, Kate had discovered that she was working in a mafia-owned restaurant and offered to be an informant for the FBI. She'd been sharp enough to figure out how to piece together the fragments of conversations she'd overheard into something useful. Especially after one of her coworkers, another waitress at the restaurant, had disappeared, only to end up floating in Lake Michigan.

He'd been ecstatic to get Kate out of there. But after they'd worked together to bring down Anthony Caruso, the state senator who was working with Salvatore, she'd flatly refused to go into a safe house.

So here she was, six months later, still in danger. And no matter what she thought, there was no way Angela would have been able to figure out anything nearly as valuable as what Kate had discovered.

As much as it pained him to admit the truth, Kate had strong investigative instincts. Somehow, he didn't think Angela was nearly as good.

"Angie might not even realize what she knows," Kate was saying. "But we can ask her questions, see if she remembers seeing Dean Ravden there, meeting with Salvatore. Putting the two of them together would be helpful."

He raised a brow. "Even if Ravden is dead?"

She scowled. "*Especially* because Ravden might be dead. First of all, we don't know for sure he was the one who died in my father's house. But if he was, then we can add that to the case we're building against Salvatore."

"Circumstantial at best," he murmured.

"It's a place to start."

He stared at the picture on the screen of the new Berkshire Racetrack. Linking Ravden's death to Salvatore might be a place to start, but somehow he knew that the new racetrack was the way to finish it.

He just needed to figure out how to accomplish that minor feat, especially now that his Tex Ryan connection to Salvatore was exposed.

Logan didn't like the thought of meeting up with Angela and Kate's brother, but he didn't think they had a choice. According to the article, the new Berkshire Racetrack was scheduled to open the following Friday night. Today was Saturday, so they had less than a week.

As part of his Tex Ryan cover, he'd given Salvatore a large sum of money to be used as an investment in the racetrack. Logan's boss was hoping the partnership would create a bond of trust, so they could find out more about Salvatore's illegal activities.

Now Logan wondered if Salvatore had established another partnership for the racetrack. Or was the mobster moving forward on his own? The racino as an investment opportunity was a sham since the payouts they were to receive for their investments would be paid with laundered money.

Logan's boss had wanted to trace the money through the process, in order to bring down Salvatore. But that wasn't going to be possible, now that his cover was blown. So they needed a plan B.

Too bad he was drawing a blank on that one.

He realized Kate was turning on her disposable phone. "What are you doing?"

She flashed him an exasperated look. "Calling my brother Garrett. I told you we're meeting up with him and Angie. I have to find out where."

"Okay, but make it quick."

She rolled her eyes in a show of annoyance, but then frowned when her call went straight to voice mail. "Garrett, it's me, Kate. I just spoke to Angie, thanks for bailing her out. Call me ASAP to let me know where you guys are meeting so I can join you."

"Do you really think he'll call?" he asked.

She stared at him. "Why wouldn't he?"

"I don't know—maybe to keep you safe?" He understood she wanted to avenge her father's death, but he wished she valued her own life just as much.

* * *

Kate volunteered to get them something to eat for lunch, mostly because sitting around while Logan did internet searches was driving her crazy.

She glanced at her phone for the zillionth time since she'd left Garrett that voice mail message. Why wasn't he calling her back? What could possibly be taking so long?

She went to the closest fast-food restaurant, the place where she'd picked up breakfast, to get a few burgers. She was tired of fast food, but it wasn't as if they could afford to get a hotel room that was equipped with a kitchen. Even if there were time to cook a meal, which there wasn't.

After she'd paid for their food, her phone rang. She pulled out from the drive-through window, juggling the food and the steering wheel. She quickly turned into a vacant parking spot and grabbed the phone, hoping it wasn't too late. "Hello? Garrett?"

"Kate, I think something has happened to Angela."

"What?" She gripped the phone tightly. "Why? What happened?"

"She was supposed to meet me thirty minutes ago, but she didn't show. And now she's not answering her phone." Garrett's voice was harsh with fear mixed with frustration. "I think Salvatore must have found her."

No! She didn't want to believe that. "I spoke to

her a few hours ago, Garrett. She was riding the subway. It could be just that it's taking her longer to get there."

"Maybe." He didn't sound the least bit hopeful. "Stay away from here, Katie, do you understand? If I find Angela, I'll let you know."

"Wait!" She didn't want her brother to hang up on her. "Why won't you tell me where you are?"

"Remember how you didn't want to get me involved? Well, the same holds true for me. I took a gamble contacting Angela, and I lost. Just stay away from here, Kate. Promise me!"

"Okay, I promise." What else could she do? It wasn't as if she could trace his cell phone to get his location. "But, Garrett, you have to keep in touch. Why didn't you answer your phone?"

"I was in the middle of something and trying to hurry so I could meet Angela. I have to go. I want to make another sweep of the area here, just to be on the safe side."

"All right, call me as soon as you hear anything." She hung up the phone and sat for a few seconds, staring blindly out through the windshield of Logan's car.

Where was Angie? Had Russo or Salvatore found her before she could get to Garrett? Or was she still hiding somewhere, trying to get to the meeting place?

She was about to put the car in gear, when she

spotted a kid on a skateboard heading toward her. She wanted to call Salvatore's restaurant but not with her own cell phone, so she opened her car door and flagged down the kid.

"What's up?" he said, eyeing her suspiciously.

"I'll give you a dollar if you let me borrow your cell phone to make a quick call."

"A dollar?" His upper lip curled in disgust. "Man, you gotta make it worth my while."

"Okay, five bucks!" She held out the bill, waiting impatiently for him to hand over the phone.

He seemed to debate whether or not he could get more, but then grudgingly handed over his smartphone.

With shaking fingers, she dialed the number for the restaurant, practically holding her breath. Was it possible Angela was there? That maybe her former roommate had planned to set up Garrett, the same way she'd done Kate?

The phone on the other end rang several times before someone picked it up. "Salvatore's, may I help you?"

She recognized the falsely polite tone of Suzanne, the hostess, who no doubt knew exactly what sort of boss she had. "May I speak with Angela Giordano?"

There was a long pause. "I'm sorry, but Ms. Giordano doesn't work here anymore."

The sharp click of Suzanne hanging up on her

seemed almost as loud as a gunshot. Numbly, she handed the cell back to the skater. "Thanks."

The kid shoved the phone in the pocket of his baggy cargo shorts and she thought he muttered "weirdo" under his breath as he skated away.

She didn't care. There were bigger issues to worry about. She slid back into Logan's car and drove as fast as she dared back to the hotel, battling another wave of helplessness.

She didn't want to believe the worst, but deep down, she knew the truth. They were too late to save Angie. Salvatore must have gotten to her.

How many more would die before they managed to arrest him?

NINE

Logan pushed away from the computer and rubbed his eyes to ease the strain. The grand opening of the brand-new racetrack was the key, but he couldn't think of a way to trap Salvatore without help.

Broodingly, he sat back in the chair and stared out the motel room window. Kate should be back any moment and he was no further ahead than when she had left to pick up lunch.

Maybe it was time to call his boss. Ken Simmons wouldn't be happy to know what happened days ago and how he was just getting around to contacting him now. But what other choice did he have? He needed help, beyond Kate. He needed resources—and not just money, although they only had enough cash to last for a few more days.

He had the listening device, but he would need to figure out how and where to plant it so that he could get the most valuable information.

Maybe at the racetrack itself? He spun back toward the computer, intent on reviewing the floor plans once again. Maybe, just maybe, there was a conference room of some sort where the "investors" would meet and discuss business. He knew that Salvatore had gone there once before, so it was possible that the mafia boss would go again.

He'd found exactly what he was looking for when Kate returned. She came in through her motel room door, carrying the bags of fast food, her expression grim. He frowned. "What's wrong?"

She set down the bag of food on the table and dropped into the empty chair. "Angie was supposed to meet my brother Garrett, but didn't show. And she doesn't work at the restaurant anymore, either. I think—Salvatore silenced her once and for all."

Kate looked so devastated, he wanted to reach over and take her into his arms. But he feared he'd be tempted to kiss her again, so he forced himself to stay where he was. "I'm sorry, Kate," he murmured, aching for her. Maybe they should have contacted Angela earlier? Although he still wasn't sure the woman could be trusted. And there were other possibilities, as well. "It could be that she's just running late, though, right?"

"I don't think so," she said wearily. "The meeting was well over an hour ago."

"But it's possible, right? Say, for instance, that she thought she was being followed? She'd go out of her way to lose a tail before going to meet your brother." It wasn't like him to offer false hope, but he couldn't stand to see Kate looking so defeated. Especially when he knew that Angela would have had a better chance to escape if he'd agreed to contact her right away, when Kate had asked him to.

"Maybe," she said, sitting up straighter in her chair. "I'm going to keep my disposable cell phone on, because Garrett promised to call if he had an update."

"No problem." He wasn't in the mood to deny her anything right now. "Let's eat before the food gets cold, okay?"

She grimaced a little, as if she didn't have much of an appetite, but reached for the hamburger bag nonetheless. He took the sandwich she held out to him, and then waited before unwrapping his food, because he knew she was going to pray. He found it unsettling the way he'd fallen into Kate's routine.

She set her burger in front of her and then closed her eyes and bowed her head. "Dear Lord, thank You for this food, we're grateful to be able to eat when others go hungry. Also, please keep Angela Giordano safe in your care and forgive whatever sins she may have committed, Amen."

"Amen." He was touched and a little amazed that she'd included Angela in her prayers. And he remembered how he'd prayed during those life-threatening moments in the cemetery. Was God really watching over them? He wished he could believe that were true, but then why had God taken Jennifer? Kate said that God always had a plan, and that they had to trust in Him, but it wasn't easy. Not when Jennifer had been young and innocent. He couldn't fathom why her life on earth had to be cut short, while he was still here.

"What are you looking at?" Kate asked between bites, her eyes glued to his computer screen. "Is that a floor plan for the Berkshire Racetrack? How did you get that?"

He dragged his thoughts away from the painful past, taking a healthy bite of his burger to ease the hunger pains in his stomach before taking the time to answer. "I still have access to the bureau's search engines." He lightly tapped the screen. "I think this room is where I'm going to plant the listening device."

Her eyebrows lifted, and he knew she was remembering how they'd used it six months ago to listen in on Salvatore's dinner conversation with the late Senator Caruso. Salvatore had all kinds of power in his back pocket. "Not a bad idea."

He munched a French fry and shrugged. "It's a long shot, but worth a try."

She sighed and nodded. "That's about all we have left, isn't it?"

"Hey, we have a lot of options left," he said, despite thinking the same thing just a few minutes ago. "Don't give up hope, Kate. We're going to nail Salvatore. He will be punished for his crimes."

"I hope so," she said softly.

They finished the rest of their meal in companionable silence. He was struck again by how nice it was to have Kate nearby to bounce around ideas with. After eating, Kate changed the dressing on his arm, and then Logan discussed plans to get the listening device inside the not-yet-opened racetrack.

"I think we should go in late at night. Fewer people around," Kate said.

"Agreed, although we'll need to make sure there aren't any security guards in place yet."

"Can you pick the lock to get inside?" she asked.

"Well, now, I'm hurt that you doubt my ability," he drawled, laying on thick his Texas accent.

When she smiled, he caught his breath and looked away. This was not the time to think about how beautiful she was. They had things to do. Plans to make.

And he couldn't afford to think about anything beyond bringing Salvatore to justice.

Logan was glad that Kate agreed to stay near the trees outside, covering him as he crept up to the Berkshire track in the darkness. The hour was well after midnight, and he was anxious to get in and out as soon as humanly possible. They were both dressed in black from head to toe, with ski masks to hide their pale faces.

There weren't guards, but there were security cameras—especially in the parking lot, in the front atop the main doors and at the back where the horse stalls were located. Messing with the security cameras would only raise suspicions, so he crouched behind a tree and used his binoculars to see if there was another way in. The proposed racino had a kitchen, nothing fancy, but enough of one to serve hot dogs, hamburgers and chicken sandwiches. Luckily, the kitchen door didn't have a security camera stationed anywhere he could see—a lapse that would work in their favor.

He stayed low, moving in the darkness until he reached the kitchen door. After picking the lock, he headed inside, imagining the floor plan in his head. The small conference room nestled between the offices was located way on the other side of the building.

There was no way to know if there were cameras inside or not, so he stayed in the darkness as much as possible, at least until he reached the conference room. Once there, he used the small penlight to find the best hiding spot. The technology used to make this listening device was state-of-the-art and wouldn't be picked up by regular bug sweepers.

He was half-afraid there wouldn't be any furniture yet, but there was a beautiful maple conference room table with six cushy chairs surrounding it. He didn't waste any time planting the bug beneath the center of the table. The moment he had it affixed, he turned off the penlight and made his way out to the kitchen, using nothing but touch.

When he slipped back outside, crossing over to where Kate was waiting, he couldn't help but grin. "Mission accomplished," he whispered.

"Thank You, Lord," she murmured. "Now let's get out of here."

He wasn't about to argue. They kept as far away from the cameras as possible as they cut across the small field to get to the hiding spot where they'd left their car.

After they had put several miles between them and the Berkshire Racetrack, he heard Kate let out a heavy sigh. "I don't think I'd like being a burglar. Too stressful."

He glanced at her. "Being a cop isn't any less stressful, you know."

"I hope you don't mind, but I'm planning to attend church in the morning," she said, completely changing the subject.

"Church?" He mentally switched gears to catch up, not surprised that she'd dodged his comment about her career. Was tomorrow, or rather, today, really Sunday? "Where?"

"There's a small church located a few miles from the motel. If you don't want me to drive, I'll walk."

He didn't like the thought of her going anywhere alone. He hadn't been in a church since he had lost Jennifer, but it looked as though he was going to break his streak by going along with Kate. "I'll go with you."

She glanced at him in surprise. "You will?"

"Yes, I will." Going to church didn't mean he was going to embrace religion the way his buddy Jonah Stewart did. Back when he was young he'd found sermons to be dull and boring, and he doubted that had changed much. But he could use the time to plan out their next move, while making sure Kate stayed safe.

Besides, it was only an hour or so. He could put up with anything for that long.

After they returned to the motel, they both retreated to their separate rooms, keeping the connecting door closed for privacy. They only had a few hours to sleep before the service Kate had chosen to attend would start.

When his radio alarm clock blared good ole country music in his ear, he groaned and turned over, wincing as he inadvertently squashed the wound on his arm. The pain had him instantly regretting his offer to go to church, if it involved getting up now. The music lightened his spirit, though. Maybe he had had to give up his cowboy boots and his Stetson, but at least he had country music to remind him of his Texas roots.

He was more than a little tempted to back out of attending the service. Kate could easily go alone. She could take the car and he'd enjoy another hour of sleep before she returned.

But even though he turned off the radio alarm clock and closed his eyes, he knew he wouldn't be able to fall back asleep. So he reluctantly got up and headed into the bathroom.

After he showered, shaved and changed the dressing on his arm, relieved to note that it didn't look infected, he went to the connecting door between their rooms. He knocked lightly, and Kate answered right away, as if she'd been waiting for him.

"Ready?" she asked. "Do you need me to change your dressing first?"

"No, I already took care of it. Let's take everything with us—we'll need to find a new place to stay, anyway." He grabbed his computer case and the few clothes he had before he followed her outside. Once they were both settled in the front seat, he started the car and headed toward the road. "Which way?"

"Left. It's just a mile or two down the road."

Sure enough, the steeple could be seen almost immediately, above the trees. He had to admit, it was a beautiful church, all white with small but colorful stained-glass windows. He was reminded of the church he'd attended as a youngster.

Once they were seated inside, the choir broke into song, and he sat listening to the music rather than using the time to plan their day.

When the pastor began his sermon, he thought for sure he'd be bored, but the subject of the sermon was everlasting life to those who believed, no doubt because of the recent Easter holiday.

"Listen as I read from Acts 11:16–18," the pastor said before looking down at his Bible. "'Then I remembered what the Lord had said: "John baptized with water, but you will be baptized with the Holy Spirit." So if God gave them the same gift he gave us who believed in the Lord Jesus Christ, who was I to think that I could stand in God's way?'"

Logan sat in stunned silence for a moment, the last few words resonating deep within. Kate was right. Who was he to think he could second-guess God's plan? Jennifer was a better person than he was. She believed in God, and as the pastor's sermon went on, he found himself listening intently.

"And we learn this from 1 John 5:12–14," the pastor said after turning to another page in the Bible. "'Whoever has the Son has life; whoever does not have the Son of God does not have life. I write these things to you who believe in the name of the Son of God so that you may know that you have eternal life. This is the confidence we have in approaching God: that if we ask anything according to his will, he hears us.'"

For the first time since losing Jennifer, Logan felt a strange sense of peace. And he understood now what Kate had been trying to tell him. That Jennifer was in a better place, up in heaven. She wasn't suffering the way he was. Maybe he'd had it backward all this time. God had chosen to bring Jennifer home, but had left him behind on purpose. To hurt and suffer.

Because he hadn't believed? Because Jennifer was a better person than he was?

The truth was suddenly very clear. So he closed his eyes and the prayer came from deep within his heart. *Dear Lord, forgive me for not understanding Your will. Please guide me along the path You've chosen for me. And please give me the strength to keep Kate safe from harm.*

Kate was amazed by how attentive Logan was during the pastor's sermon. She'd expected him to either look bored or preoccupied with Salvatore.

Yet he was following along with the Bible readings, as if discovering them for the first time. He had mentioned his parents taking him to church as a child, but he'd made it clear that he hadn't sustained a close relationship with God over the years.

Especially after losing his fiancée.

Yet here he was standing beside her, Bible in

hand. She was pleased that he'd not only attended church with her today, but appeared to be taking the sermon to heart.

Or was that nothing more than wishful thinking?

She hoped not, because she ached for him. For his loss, so similar to her own. The sermon was exactly what she needed to cherish her father's memory.

"Lastly, my friends, I leave you with this final word from the book of Psalms, Chapter 91, Verse 1. 'Whoever dwells in the shelter of the Most High will rest in the shadow of the Almighty.' Now please join me in reciting the Lord's Prayer."

Logan took her hand and she couldn't help reveling in the warmth of his fingers surrounding hers as they prayed together. And once the sermon was finished, she wrapped her arms around him in a brief hug. "Thank you for coming with me today, Logan. Attending church today was exactly what I needed."

"My pleasure," he murmured, returning her hug and keeping ahold of her hand as they walked back outside. She squinted a bit in the bright sunlight, even as she enjoyed the warmth against her skin.

Her smile widened as he held open the passenger door for her. "My dad would always hold a door for me," she said as she slid inside the stuffy car. After the sermon, she could think of her father without the crippling grief that had haunted her since he'd died.

"My mother drilled manners into me and my brother," he said, turning on the car and opening the windows to let out the stifling heat while she buckled her seat belt. "Old habits are hard to break."

She was glad, and wanted to tell Logan how much her father, if he'd still been alive, would like him. But she kept her thoughts to herself, afraid of making him uncomfortable and breaking the sense of camaraderie that had settled between them.

As Logan steered the car out of the church parking lot and back onto the highway, she noticed a tan car parked on the side of the road, the driver's head buried in a map. When they'd passed him, though, she noticed he instantly set aside the map and then pulled out behind them.

Immediately, the tiny hairs on the back of her neck rose in alarm. "Um, Logan? Check out the tan car behind us."

"I see him," Logan said, although his gaze didn't lift up to the rearview mirror. "If he's really following us, then I'll lose him."

She tried not to stare into her side-view mirror at the car behind them, but it wasn't easy. "I don't understand. How could they possibly have found us?"

"Good question. Tracking our disposable cell

phones would be nearly impossible, since I paid for them with cash."

Her stomach churned. "I didn't turn mine off last night," she confessed softly. "I was waiting to hear good news from Garrett and forgot about it."

He glanced at her, but didn't look angry. "As I said, it would be hard to trace us through the disposable cell phones. A more likely scenario is that someone spotted our car last night, during our visit to the Berkshire Racetrack."

"How? You told me this car couldn't be traced to you, and besides, we parked far away from the cameras," she protested.

"I don't know," Logan said grimly. He turned onto a less-used country road, and the car behind them followed.

The knot of dread in her stomach tightened painfully. "I don't like this, Logan. What if that guy is another of Salvatore's goons?"

"Don't worry, I'll keep you safe."

She braced herself by holding on to the door handle, but he didn't increase the speed of the car. In fact, Logan acted as if they didn't have anywhere pressing to go.

She told herself to take deep breaths, relax and trust in Logan's experience, but it wasn't easy. The country highway they'd taken twisted and turned but there wasn't any traffic, so the car following exactly two car lengths behind them was only that much more noticeable.

It couldn't be good that the guy didn't even try to hide the fact that he was on their tail. Was he planning on killing them both in the bright light of day?

Without warning, Logan stomped on the brakes and yanked the steering wheel to the right, tires squealing as he turned onto a dirt road that disappeared into a wooded area that looked to be private property.

"What are you doing?" she squeaked.

"Get out!" He slammed on the brakes and opened the driver's-side door the same time she opened hers. "This way." He came around the car, grabbed her hand and pulled her into the trees just thirty seconds before she heard the sound of the second car turning down the same dirt road.

She barely had time to think as Logan pushed her down into the bushes, hiding her from view. He pulled out his weapon, which he must have been carrying even while they were in church, she realized grimly. He kept his hand on her back as he crouched beside her, waiting for Salvatore's goon to come after them.

TEN

Kate struggled to control her breathing so that she wouldn't inadvertently give away their location. She concentrated on listening, and after the other car's engine stopped, she heard the soft *snick* as the driver opened the car door.

Every muscle in her body tensed. She trusted Logan, but the impending danger made her acutely aware of the vulnerability of their position. The guy in the tan car was the hunter and they were the prey.

Logan remained motionless beside her, his gaze intent as he stared through the brush. And then slowly, very slowly, she saw him raise his weapon.

She grabbed his arm. "Don't," she whispered urgently. She couldn't bear the thought of Logan shooting the guy following them in cold blood.

But then she heard a gunshot and ducked as the tree branches rustled overhead.

Logan returned fire and she heard a soft cry, indicating Logan had hit his target.

"Stay here," he whispered, but she clutched his arm, preventing him from leaving. "I wasn't shooting to kill, I only wanted to wound him. I need to know who sent him after us."

"No. We either stay here together or we move forward together."

A look of impatience flashed across his face at the same time they heard the sound of a car engine.

"He's getting away," Logan said, yanking from her grasp and charging out of the brush. She pushed aside the leaves and branches, staying right behind him, instinctively knowing that Logan would want her to follow. When they reached the dirt road, the other car was gone.

Without a word, she jumped in the passenger seat and closed the door as Logan went around to the driver's side. Within moments he backed out of the dirt road, while she kept an eye out for the tan car. She was very much afraid that the guy would pull the same trick they'd just performed, hiding and waiting for them to show themselves.

She needn't have worried, because by the time they reached the paved road, there wasn't any sign of the other car. The country road took a curve about a mile to the right, so she wasn't surprised when Logan headed that way.

"Do you know where you hit him?" she asked.

"Somewhere along his right side," Logan said. "My goal was to get him to talk." He eased up on the gas as they went around the curve, only to see a fork in the road up ahead.

He brought the car to a stop at the intersection, but even looking both ways, she couldn't see any sign of the tan car. "I can't believe we lost him," she muttered.

"Me, either," Logan admitted. "If I'd have known there was an intersection this close, I would have kept going."

She reached out to put a hand on his arm. "He got lucky, that's all. I don't suppose there's any hope he would get treated at a hospital and we should alert the local authorities?"

"Maybe. I have to call my boss anyway," he said slowly. "Although if the guy works for Salvatore, then there's a chance he'll be able to get medical treatment from someone on the mafia's payroll."

The idea was frustrating beyond belief. "Does he have someone from every profession in his pocket?" she asked harshly. "Doctors are supposed to uphold their Hippocratic oath. They shouldn't be swayed by criminals."

Logan didn't respond right away as he turned the car around in the intersection and headed back the way they'd come. "Money and power go hand in hand, remember?"

She did remember, but that didn't mean she had to like it. She sat back in her seat and let out a heavy sigh. It was easy to see why cops eventually became jaded and callous. For every crook they put away, there were dozens more to take their place.

Which made her only more determined to join the fight—as a police officer. Just like her dad and her brothers. She was convinced this was the work she was meant to do. Once she and Logan were safely out of this mess, she would try out for the police academy.

And refuse to consider failure an option.

Logan headed west, intending to find a place to stay on the other side of the racetrack. As he drove, he kept a sharp eye on the road behind them, hoping they wouldn't pick up another tail. The fact that someone had managed to follow them to church had badly shaken him. He couldn't stand the idea of Kate being in danger.

As soon as they'd found a motel, he'd call his boss. Enough of trying to do this on their own. That had been a close call back there. If he hadn't taken everything out of the motel room, including his weapon, the situation could have turned out very differently.

He wasn't sure the guy he'd hit would have told them much, but he felt certain the puppet master pulling the strings had to be Salvatore. Still, something about this latest scenario didn't quite add up.

He searched his memory, retracing their steps outside the racetrack. They'd stayed away from the cameras, but had there been others that he'd missed? Or had they been followed even last night? But if so, there's no way he would have gotten inside the building. He and Kate hadn't been in a hurry at all. In fact, they'd taken extra precautions to make sure that they wouldn't be discovered. Plenty of time for someone to take them out, if they had in fact been followed.

No, that scenario didn't play for him. Which left only two options: that somehow they had been on a hidden camera, or someone was tracking Officer Gerlach's phone, even though it was mostly turned off.

Neither option was particularly reassuring.

And regardless of who had come after them, one thing was certain. Their vehicle was compromised. They needed a new set of wheels, the sooner the better.

Too bad he wasn't sure how to get what they needed.

About three hours later, he found the perfect motel, just ten miles away from the Berkshire Racetrack. He rented two rooms for him and Kate, and then placed the call to his boss.

"Where have you been?" Simmons demanded. "You've missed several check-ins!"

"I know. Things have gone downhill in a big way." He tried to think of a way to soften the news, but couldn't come up with one. "My Tex Ryan cover is blown. Salvatore has set his goons after me."

There was a long silence and he could almost imagine the fury that was etched in his boss's craggy features. "What happened?"

The last thing he wanted to do was talk about it, especially since Kate had come into the room. He glanced at her and flashed a lopsided smile. "Look, a lot has happened, and there isn't time to go over everything right now. You need to put out an alert with the area hospitals. I wounded a guy following me earlier today. I also need a new set of wheels, and more cash. Can we meet somewhere?"

"More cash?" He could hear the tense anger vibrating in his boss's tone. "Do you have any idea how much money we've wasted on this investigation so far? And what do we have to show for it? Nothing. Nada. Zip! Logan, you blew your cover!"

Ken Simmons didn't understand that Logan felt guilty enough. Adding more wasn't going to make a difference. "I have something," he protested, even though he knew the argument was weak. "I was able to plant the high-tech bug in the conference room of the new racetrack. If Salvatore holds another meeting there, we'll be ready."

"If? *If?*" Simmons's tone rose, incredulous. "I'm supposed to bank on a long shot? Is that what you're telling me?"

He pulled the phone away from his ear with a wince. "Get me new transpo. Something that can't be traced. Help me out, and I will get you the evidence you need to bring Salvatore down."

"You'd better," Simmons said in a threatening tone. "Because if I go down because you bungled this job, then you're going with me."

"I know." He wouldn't have expected anything else. "When and where can we meet?"

"Are you in Chicago? Or closer to the racetrack?"

"Let's pick someplace halfway in between," he suggested, sidestepping his boss's question. They weren't far from Chicago Midway International Airport, but he didn't want to give out his exact location. He searched his memory. "There's a statue of Louis Armstrong in the center of Maplesville Park. Send someone to meet me there. With cash and keys."

"Maplesville Park? Okay, but it's going to take some time. I probably can't get anyone there until seven o'clock this evening."

He glanced at his watch, surprised to realize it was already almost three in the afternoon. "No problem. Seven is perfect."

"Don't mess this up, Quail," his boss muttered. "Neither of us can afford to fail."

"I hear you." He disconnected the call and glanced at Kate, who'd been listening to his side of the conversation. "He's not very happy with me, but he'll come through with what we need."

"I figured as much. I'm starving. Do we have time to eat before we meet him at the park?"

He stifled a sigh as he turned to unpack his computer case. "I don't suppose I can convince you to stay here and wait for me?"

"No, you can't. We're a team, Logan. So far that's been working out well for us, hasn't it?" Her green-brown Irish-mud eyes implored him to agree.

He didn't want to admit she was right. Not when their recent near escape was still so fresh in his mind. But he'd worry about her, whether she was here waiting for him or not, so he might as well keep her close. "Yeah, sure." He paused and then added, "Give me a few minutes to check the various routes on the computer, and then we'll go. We'll have time to stop and get something to eat. I want to arrive at the park early, to make sure everything is on the up-and-up."

Her eyes widened in surprise. "Surely you don't believe your boss would set us up?"

"There is no *us,* as far as he knows. I didn't tell him about you, as there will be plenty of time for that later. And no, I don't think he'd compromise us. I'm trusting him to bring me a new vehicle and some cash. But I'm not willing to go in blind, either. There's always a risk." He couldn't deny he'd become highly suspicious of everyone and everything over the six months he'd been working on the Salvatore case. Maybe because he'd seen more than a few important people who'd aligned themselves with criminals, like State Senator Anthony Caruso and the Milwaukee chief of police. No one was immune, and he wasn't about to take any chances.

Especially not with Kate's life.

Kate stared down at her phone, which she'd turned off after their near miss with the guy who'd followed them after church. She hadn't heard from Garrett and she was certain that couldn't be good.

Had she put Garrett in danger, too? He'd told her to stay away from him, so she had to think so. Although she certainly hadn't told him to get ahold of Angela Giordano, either.

She wasn't sure why Garrett had contacted her former roommate, but it was probably to get them inside information on Salvatore. She could imagine Garrett getting frustrated with being unable to help Angie and deciding to work the case from another angle.

Nibbling her lower lip, she pushed the button to turn on her phone. The small screen lit up and she practically held her breath as she waited to see if there was a voice mail message or text waiting for her.

But there was nothing. Since Logan was preoccupied with staring at the map of Maplesville Park, she sent a quick text message.

AG show up yet?

There was a long pause, and she was about to turn off her phone again, when her brother responded.

No. Where r u?

She couldn't tell him, so she avoided his question.

Safe, but can't talk, will call later.

Turning off her phone was difficult when she would have given anything to see her brother. Or at least talk to him, hear the sound of his voice. Being isolated like this, away from her family, was horrible.

But temporary. Something she needed to remember. Something to hold on to.

"Ready?" Logan asked, straightening from the computer. She belatedly realized he was in the process of shutting down the machine.

"Yes." She ignored her emotional and physical exhaustion. "Are you bringing the computer along?"

"Bring everything. We'll be exchanging vehicles."

"Which means we'll need to find a new place to stay." It shouldn't matter, but this constant changing of motel rooms was wearing on her.

"Afraid so." Logan slung the computer case over his shoulder and held open the door. "Don't worry. We'll find something just as convenient."

She nodded and followed him outside. "How about we eat at that Mexican place we passed on the way here?"

He grinned. "Why not? Mexican it is."

Kate sat back in her chair with a groan. "I should have stopped at two burritos," she moaned.

He chuckled and pushed away his plate. "I'm stuffed, too. But I'm afraid we need to get going."

"I'm ready when you are."

The waitress came at Logan's signal and handed them the bill. She winced when she saw Logan's dwindling amount of cash. "Do we have enough?"

"We're fine." He tossed down the bills and stood. "Come on, let's hit the road."

The drive to Maplesville Park took a good hour and a half. But they still had almost another hour before their scheduled meeting. Dark clouds swirled in the sky, and she watched them warily, hoping the rain would hold off until after they had their new vehicle and more cash.

Logan insisted on parking far away and walking in from the south. Since she hadn't studied the map the way he had, she didn't argue. As they walked along the sidewalks, she noticed that there weren't many people around. She saw one jogger, heading past them as if on the way home, and a couple kids on Rollerblade skates.

She pulled together her hoodie, as the temperature had dropped. A storm threatened. They walked past the bronze statue of Louis Armstrong, the famous jazz musician, to make their way through the rest of the park.

There was nothing remotely suspicious anywhere, but she was still tense, unable to get rid of the strange sense of heightened awareness.

"Let's sit here for a moment," Logan said, interrupting her thoughts as he gestured to a park bench. "And then I'd like you to go back and wait for me in the car."

"No way." She glared at him. "If you don't want your boss to see me, I'll hide. There was a good-sized tree not far from the statue. I'll keep watch for anything out of the ordinary."

"We've just gone through the entire park. I think we're as safe as can be."

How could she explain her deep sense of foreboding? "Please? I'll go crazy sitting in the car."

"All right, you can sit behind the tree. But you'll have to go now and you'll be tired and cramped being there for the next twenty minutes or so."

"I don't care." She was willing to do whatever

was necessary to keep him safe. "I'll go now, and make sure no one sees me."

There was the slight rumble of thunder in the distance, and Logan grimaced. "I doubt we'll have to worry about that—everyone will be heading home to beat the storm."

Everyone except the two of them. She gave him a fleeting smile, and then rose to her feet and ambled down the sidewalk, back toward the statue.

She didn't pass anyone on her way back, and it was easy enough to slip off the sidewalk, cutting through the wooded area until she reached the large oak tree. She walked around it, checking several spots for the best view, before she hunkered down, making herself comfortable. She glanced at her watch and grimaced. Still eighteen minutes before the scheduled meeting time.

Patience wasn't exactly her strong suit.

After ten minutes, her legs started to go numb so she shifted a bit, making sure she didn't make any noise. She removed the large rock from beneath her hip, and immediately felt much better. It wouldn't do Logan any good if she were physically unable to help him. Or to run.

Another four minutes passed before she saw Logan slowly approach the bronze statue from the area to her left. She was glad she'd kept the tree to her right so she could easily keep him in view.

Out of the corner of her eye, she saw something

move. She eased from behind the tree, trying to get a better view. There was an old homeless guy, dressed in multiple layers of clothing, a tattered hat pulled low over his eyes, pushing an old rusty grocery cart.

As she watched him, she noticed he was muttering to himself under his breath, his shoulder twitching every few minutes.

He was likely harmless, but the uneasy feeling that she'd had ever since arriving at the park was growing stronger. She knew she should be watching Logan, waiting for either his boss or someone else from the FBI task force to show up, but she couldn't seem to tear her gaze from the homeless guy.

The shopping cart hit a rock, and teetered precariously. The homeless guy grabbed it, preventing the cart from toppling over and spilling all his worldly possessions on the ground.

In that instant she saw a flash of silver on his wrist. A watch? On a homeless guy?

Her heart leaped into her throat. She picked up the rock she'd dug out of the ground a few minutes ago, and abruptly stood. "Watch out!" she shouted to Logan, before lobbing the rock toward the homeless guy.

She managed to hit her target in the shoulder, and he flinched away from the impact, even as

Logan dove behind the statue. The homeless guy straightened and that's when she saw it.

"He has a gun!" she shouted, drawing the fake homeless guy's attention from Logan to herself. He swung the weapon toward her at the same time Logan popped his head up from behind the statue and took aim.

She ducked behind the tree, as the sound of gunfire echoed through the night.

ELEVEN

Dear Lord, keep Logan safe! Kate prayed as she pressed her back against the tree. She should have looked for more rocks, or branches—anything to use as a weapon. Another crack of thunder rumbled above, followed by an abrupt downpour of rain.

The leaves on the tree above protected her somewhat, but not enough to keep her dry. She listened, trying to figure out what was happening with Logan and the guy in disguise. She heard the rustle of leaves from her left and tensed, only to relax when she recognized Logan.

Thank You, Lord!

"Are you all right?" he asked harshly.

"Yes. What about the fake homeless guy?" She could tell, by the grim expression etched in Logan's features, the news wouldn't be good.

"He's still alive, but I'm not sure for how long. He moved as I was shooting and I ended up hitting him in the stomach. We need to get out of here."

She peeled herself away from the tree, her skin indented from the pattern of the bark. He put his arm around her shoulders and she leaned gratefully against him for a moment.

"Can you walk?" he asked with concern.

"Of course I can walk." She told herself to stop being a wimp, and moved away from Logan. "Did your contact show up from the FBI?" she asked as they made their way back out of the park to where they'd left the car.

"I think I saw him, his name is Jerry Kahler, but the moment you yelled he took off in the other direction." The fierce expression on his face matched his frustrated tone. "So close."

Too close. She couldn't help thinking about what might have happened if she hadn't noticed the flash of silver on the gunman's wrist.

"This way," Logan said, tugging on her hand.

She frowned. "Our car is this way." She pointed in the opposite direction.

"I know, but I'm looking for the vehicle left by the fake homeless guy. It has to be somewhere close to the park."

"How do you know he left a car?" she demanded. "And I have to call 9-1-1, Logan. He needs medical attention."

"I put a pressure bandage on his wound, so he'll be okay for a few minutes. We'll call 9-1-1 as soon as we find his car."

She kept pace with him as best she could, but the rain made it difficult to see very well. Just when she thought that maybe they were lost, she heard Logan say, "Yes! There it is."

She didn't see anything, until the headlights flickered and she heard a beep. She turned to look at Logan. "You found his keys?"

"And a bit of cash, but no wallet or ID," he said as they approached the car. "Stay back, in case it's wired."

"Wired?" She wiped the water from her eyes. "You mean like with a bomb?" Was he crazy? "Logan, don't—"

"Just give me a few minutes, okay?" he interrupted. She stood uncertainly as he pulled out a small penlight and then dropped to the ground to crawl under the vehicle.

She was soaked to the skin and now that the adrenaline had worn off, she began to shiver, almost uncontrollably. She hugged herself and lightly jogged in place in an attempt to stay warm. After what seemed like forever, but was probably less than ten minutes, Logan scooted back out from beneath the car and motioned her over. Now that she was closer, she realized it was an SUV.

"It's clean. I've already disabled the GPS. Come on, let's get inside."

She wasn't going to argue. Being out of the rain helped, but she was still freezing. As if he could read her mind, Logan put the key in the ignition, turned on the motor and then cranked the heat on high.

"You'd better call 9-1-1 for the guy back there," he said as he pulled away from the curb. "I'm going to get our stuff, and then we're getting far away from here."

She nodded, forcing her frozen fingers to push the buttons on the phone. When the dispatcher came on the line, asking what her emergency was, she took a deep breath. "There's a man with a gunshot wound in Maplesville Park near the Louis Armstrong statue in the center. Please hurry."

"Wait, don't hang up…" the dispatcher started to say, but Kate pushed the end-call button regardless, knowing that the dispatcher would still send a squad to check it out.

"They're going to have your voice on tape," Logan pointed out.

"And my cell number." As much as she hated to admit it, she'd need to ditch the phone. With a sigh, she opened the window of the SUV and tossed out the disposable phone, barely able to hear the *ping* as it hit the ground.

Within a few minutes, he'd pulled up to the car they'd left behind. "Wait here," he said before getting out.

It didn't take him long to grab their stuff from the vehicle, stashing the computer case and their clothes into the backseat of the SUV. He tossed a sweatshirt in her lap. "Use this to warm up."

She did, even though putting it on over her wet clothes would only get the sweatshirt damp, too. They'd have to find a motel with a laundry, she thought with a weary sigh as Logan headed north.

"Now what?" she asked, feeling depressed. "Where do we go from here?"

Logan didn't answer right away. "I need help, and clearly going back to my boss isn't an option."

"You don't think your boss turned on you, do you?"

He shrugged. "I don't know what to think. But I can't trust that it wouldn't happen again."

She could see his point. "Do you want to call my brother Garrett?" she offered.

"No, but there's a Chicago Detective that I worked with six months ago, a guy named Nick Butler. He knows about Salvatore because he worked on a related missing person case."

She tried not to feel hurt that Logan would prefer to use this Nick Butler's help rather than her brother's, but it wasn't easy. "If that's true, why haven't we contacted Nick Butler before now?" she asked.

Logan scrubbed his hand over his jaw. "It's not like I'm anxious to call him, Kate," he said, a sharp edge to his tone. "Do you think I want to put anyone else in danger? I don't want to draw your brother or Nick Butler into this, but I don't have a choice. We need help. And Butler is one of the few guys I can trust."

Now that he put it that way, she could admit she didn't want to pull her brother further into this mess, either. She wanted her family safe from harm. She didn't know Nick Butler, but for some reason, she'd rather he be included instead of Garrett.

She frowned when Logan made a fast right-hand turn into a busy truck stop, dragging her attention from her brothers.

"Gotta change plates. Give me a sec," he explained as he parked out back in a dark area and again suffered the rain.

"By the way, nice aim back there," Logan said as he reentered the vehicle. "That's the second time you hit exactly what you were aiming at. First in the cemetery and now here. Thanks to you, he was knocked off balance."

She couldn't help but grin. "I played four years of fast-pitch softball in high school," she admitted. Pride was a sin but she couldn't help but add, "We went to state my senior year and I pitched the winning game."

"Hard to imagine you playing sports," Logan drawled. Meanwhile, he dug in his computer case, pulled out a roll of black electrical tape. Ripped off a few inches.

She lifted a brow. "Why not? My brothers were

all involved in sports, and I wanted to follow in their footsteps. I was too short to be any good at basketball and volleyball, but I found my niche with softball. We had a lot of fun."

He felt along the steering column, felt the raised impression of the VIN and placed the tape over it. Logan's answering smile made her heart flutter in her chest. "I owe you for saving my hide," he said quietly. "Thank you."

"No thanks necessary," she replied lightly. "You've saved me several times. I'm simply returning the favor."

He nodded thoughtfully and reached out to take her hand in his, gently wrapping his fingers around hers. "I was praying like I've never prayed before back there," he confessed.

"Really?" The news warmed her more than the heat blasting from the vents. "I'm so glad, Logan."

"Me, too."

She smiled and looked down at their clasped hands for a long moment, before relaxing back in her seat. She didn't pull away her hand.

And neither did Logan.

Logan found another small motel a little farther from the racetrack than he wanted, but was satisfied that no one would find them this far off the highway. He pulled up in front of the lobby and reluctantly released Kate's hand, wondering why he'd felt the need to tell her about how he'd prayed back at the park. He wasn't normally one to bare his soul to anyone, and especially not to a woman.

But Kate wasn't just any woman. The more time he spent with her, the more he liked her. Admired her. And was grateful she'd been a star player on her high school softball team. Throwing that rock at the guy had given him the time he needed to duck for cover.

God's will? Or pure luck?

Surprisingly, he was leaning toward the former.

"I'll be right back," he said as he climbed out of the SUV. He felt guilty for taking it even though it belonged to a guy who'd tried to kill him.

He paid for connecting rooms and went back to where Kate was waiting in the SUV. He drove around to park near their rooms. He reached back to grab the computer case, and the action caused the skin around his arm wound to pull sharply. Instantly, he felt something warm trickling down his arm.

"You're bleeding again," Kate said, grabbing a spare T-shirt to wrap around his arm. "Luckily we still have gauze and antibiotic ointment left."

"I'll be fine," he said gruffly.

"Don't be stubborn, Logan. You should have let me check it out this morning."

From what he could see of the wound, it had been scabbing over nicely—no doubt his actions today had helped open it again. But the wound wasn't anything serious. He'd suffered far worse in his career. There was no reason to let Kate hover over him.

No matter how much he liked it.

"Sit down," she said, after they'd gotten settled into their respective rooms.

Realizing she wouldn't relent, he gave in and sat in the chair. She'd already had fresh towels, warm water and their first-aid supplies set out on the small table. He let her unwrap the blood-soaked bandage, trying to ignore the fact that they were still sopping wet from the storm.

"I don't suppose this place has a Laundromat?" she asked as she worked.

"No, they don't. Just set your wet clothes over the wall heater. They'll be dry by morning."

She wrinkled her nose. "I guess that will have to work," she agreed. Using the washcloth, she cleaned his wound and then dried it with a towel. "This doesn't look too bad," she said as she spread more antibiotic cream over the area. "Although it would look better if you hadn't ripped off half the scab."

"I'll try to keep that in mind," he murmured drily.

She wrapped gauze around his arm and then stepped back to clean up the mess. He rose to his feet, keeping his arm at an awkward angle to prevent it from brushing against his damp shirt.

He tried to step around her, but at the same moment she turned the same way, causing them to collide. He steadied her, lightly grasping her shoulders. "Sorry," he murmured.

"Oh, Logan," she whispered, before wrapping her arms around his waist and hugging him. "I'm so glad you're all right."

"Hey, now, what's this?" he asked, alarmed by the uncharacteristic display of emotion. "Don't cry, Kate. He didn't even get close to hitting me."

"I keep seeing his gun," she muttered against his chest. "If I hadn't caught a glimpse of his watch…"

"Shh, it's all right." He tightened the embrace, ignoring the fact that he was getting his dry bandage damp again from her clothing. "You were awesome back there, Kate. You truly saved my life."

"I was so scared," she admitted. "How am I going to be a cop if I'm afraid?"

It was on the tip of his tongue to tell her to drop the whole idea of being a police officer, but he held back. Because in that moment back in the park, when she'd thrown the rock at the homeless guy with dead-center accuracy, shouting a warning at him, he had realized she'd be a great cop. She had uncanny instincts and hadn't hesitated to act.

"What makes you think cops aren't afraid?"

he asked instead. "Being fearless would make a cop reckless. All police officers are afraid at some point. But they rely on their skills and training. You haven't even attended the police academy yet, and you already have great instincts." He rubbed a hand down her back. "Instincts that you probably inherited from your dad."

She lifted her head and leaned back to look up at him. "Do you really think so?" she asked, her gaze full of hope.

"Yes, Kate. I do." And because she was so brave, and so incredibly beautiful, and because he couldn't stop himself, he leaned down and kissed her.

Kate soaked in the warmth of Logan's mouth against hers, locking her knees to keep them from buckling.

Her heart swelled with hope and longing. For the first time since they'd met over six months ago, Logan seemed to understand exactly who she was. He wasn't trying to make her into something else. He'd told her she had great instincts. Cop instincts.

Just like her father.

She kissed him back, trying to put her feelings into words. He groaned low in his throat, deepened the kiss, making her toes curl. But then he pulled away, gasping for breath.

"You're dangerous, woman," Logan said in a

low voice. "But I have to call Butler, before it gets too late."

Of course he did. They were still running for their lives, unable to figure out who they could trust.

But she wanted to linger in his arms, drawing in his heat and his strength.

"Kate?" he asked, tipping up her chin so that she met his gaze. "Are you all right?"

She forced herself to step away, flashing him a wry smile. "I'm okay. Didn't mean to cling like a vine. You'd better call your detective friend. Actually, I'm anxious to hear what he has to say."

He held her gaze for a long moment before turning away. "I hope he still has the same cell number."

She hoped so, too. While Logan made his call, she quickly cleaned up the small table, dumping out the warm, soapy water and rinsing the blood from the washcloth and towel before hanging them up to dry.

When she emerged from the bathroom, Logan was already off the phone. "He didn't answer?"

"I left a message." He shrugged and tossed the phone on the bedside table. "It's probably better that we get some sleep anyway—we'll have plenty of time to talk to Nick tomorrow."

"All right." She understood that was her cue to

return to her own room. "Good night, Logan. Let me know if you hear from Detective Butler."

"I will. Good night, Kate."

She slipped through the connecting doorways, closing her side before she shimmied out of her wet clothes and draped them over the heater to dry, as Logan had suggested. She wrapped up in the blanket from the bed and closed her eyes, willing herself to relax.

But graphic images from the park kept replaying over and over in her mind, like a horror movie.

So she turned to prayer, reciting the Lord's Prayer over and over until she finally drifted off to sleep.

The next morning she was thrilled to see that her clothes were dry, if rather wrinkly. She hung them in the bathroom, hoping the steam would help make them look better. After a quick shower, she dressed and dried her hair before going over to knock on the connecting door. "Logan? Are you awake?"

He opened the door, and she quickly realized he wasn't alone. Behind him stood a tall, broad-shouldered man with sandy-brown hair and piercing blue eyes. "Kate, this is Detective Nick Butler. Nick, this is Kate Townsend."

"Pleased to meet you," Nick said, stepping forward to shake her hand. "Any relation to Burke Townsend?"

"Yes, he was my father." She knew her smile had dimmed, but thanks to yesterday's church sermon, she didn't feel like bursting into tears.

"I'm very sorry for your loss," Nick said somberly. "He was a great cop."

"Thank you." Her stomach rumbled and she caught sight of a bag of giant muffins on the table. "You brought breakfast?"

"On the Feeb's orders," Nick teased, waving a hand toward them. "Please, help yourself."

She knew from her dad and her brothers that *Feeb* was slang for federal agent, and she couldn't help smile. "Feeb, huh? Haven't heard that term recently."

"He's just jealous because he couldn't get into Quantico," Logan drawled, his Southern accent seemingly more pronounced. "He knows that's where the best of the best end up, right, Butler?"

"Yeah, right," Butler agreed sarcastically.

She stepped closer to the table and helped herself to a chocolate-chip muffin. "Delicious," she murmured after the first bite.

"I called all the hospitals in a hundred-mile radius," Nick said, getting back to the conversation she'd interrupted. "No suspicious reports of gunshot wounds."

"I can't believe there haven't been any gunshot

wounds," she argued with a frown. "That's just not possible."

"There were plenty of gunshot wounds, just none brought in without being accompanied by law enforcement."

So no leads on the guy who'd followed them from church. "I called 9-1-1 on the fake homeless guy," she said, turning to Logan. "He would have been brought in with law enforcement, right?"

"Right." Logan glanced at Nick. "Which hospital would a victim go to after being shot in Maplesville Park?"

"Northwestern University," Nick said as he reached for his phone. "I'll check to see if they brought anyone in after seven last night."

She finished her muffin and washed it down with a large glass of water. What she wouldn't give for a tall glass of freshly squeezed orange juice.

After several long minutes, Nick finally got off the phone. "Those privacy laws are a hassle, but I did find out that they brought a guy in last night, about seven-thirty. He went straight to surgery and his condition is listed as critical."

Critical. The muffin she'd eaten suddenly felt like a rock, expanding in her stomach. "Do you think he'll survive?"

"No way to know, not without visiting, which would be impossible considering we don't know his name. We can't just show up at the hospital, asking to see the guy who was shot in the park."

"No, I guess not." She glanced at Logan, not surprised by his grim expression. He'd shot in self-defense, but she wasn't sure that would make him feel any better.

"I think I need to contact Salvatore directly," Logan announced.

Her jaw dropped at his abrupt declaration. "What? Have you lost your mind?"

Logan's tawny eyes locked on hers. "It's time to end this, Kate. And if that means offering myself up as bait, then so be it. As long as we bring down Salvatore."

But she cared! No. No way. She wasn't going to allow Logan to be bait.

Not when she knew she was losing her heart to him.

TWELVE

"Logan, don't do this," she begged, hoping to carve through the emotion he must be feeling to find cool, clear logic. "We'll find another way, won't we, Nick?"

"Absolutely," the detective agreed.

But a fiercely stubborn expression had settled over Logan's features. "I know Salvatore, better than either of you. He'll draw out this cat-and-mouse game for months if not years. He has a lot of important people under his control. You need to listen to my plan before you reject it outright."

Kate didn't want to listen to his plan. She couldn't bear to have Logan exposed for Salvatore to come after. But she could see the acceptance in Nick Butler's eyes, and knew she didn't stand a chance if he agreed with Logan.

"All right, I'll consider your plan. What are you thinking?" Butler asked.

"I'll call Salvatore and offer to sell him the high-tech bug," Logan said firmly.

"And what makes you think Salvatore will agree to buy it? Or believe that it even exists?" she challenged.

Logan glanced at her, and she caught a flash of pure agony in his gaze, before it disappeared. "For one thing, I'll be able to prove it existed, as I used it to eavesdrop on Salvatore's conversations with Russo. And second, he may not care if it truly exists, as long as he gets the opportunity to find me and kill me."

"And what is the point of that?" she demanded harshly. "Suicide by Salvatore?"

He narrowed his gaze, and she realized she may have gone a little too far. But what he was proposing did resemble a suicide mission, and she wasn't going to sit there while he offered himself up to Salvatore on a platter. "No, despite what you're obviously thinking, I'm not trying to get myself killed. I'm trying to trap Salvatore, so that we can nail him once and for all, before he kills anyone else."

His declaration made her feel a little better, but she still didn't like it. She especially didn't like the way Logan seemed intent on distancing himself from her.

Because he didn't trust her? He'd thanked her for saving his life, but that previous gratitude seemed to have evaporated. Now he was in full agent mode. Making it clear she didn't belong.

Giving her the impression that he might just walk away again, the same way he had six months ago.

"Maybe if we time this right, we can make it work," Nick agreed. "Say the evening of the grand opening of the Berkshire Racetrack?"

A small smile played along the edges of Logan's mouth. "Yeah, that's exactly what I was thinking. We'll listen in on the bug I planted and see if we can get anything useful. I'll contact Salvatore early that Friday to arrange for the sale of the device to take place after the race is finished."

"How are you planning on getting it out of the conference room?" she asked.

Logan shrugged. "I may not have to. If we can get enough on him, we'll be able to arrest him."

She stared at him incredulously. He was making it sound far too easy. "And if we don't?"

Logan avoided her gaze. "Then we'll have to wait until he tries to kill me."

Logan tried to hide a wince, as disapproval radiated off Kate in nearly tangible waves. He resisted the urge to cross over, take her into his arms to offer comfort and reassurance.

"Fine, if you're so determined to do this, you'll need body armor," she said in a clipped, irritated tone. "And even then, it's a stretch to think we can make this work, with only me and Nick backing you up."

He let out a soundless sigh. "Kate, you can't. You're not a cop."

The hurt that shadowed her gaze made him want to take back the words. "What happened to those cop instincts you claimed I had?" she asked.

"It's not that you aren't capable," he hastened to reassure her. "But you're not a cop, which means you can't legally carry a gun."

"Actually, I do have a permit to carry," she said. "My father often took me to the shooting range."

He couldn't hide his surprise. "Okay, maybe you do have a permit to carry a weapon, but don't you understand that you could be charged with a crime if you end up shooting Salvatore or one of his men?"

"I'm fairly certain I can shoot in self-defense, or in defending someone else," she replied calmly. "And who says I have to shoot anyone? Just the threat of having a gun might be enough to tip the balance in our favor."

"No way. I'm sorry, Kate, but I'm not going to allow you to do that." The very idea made his blood congeal.

"Hold on, Logan," Nick said, interrupting them. "Back up a minute. Why can't Kate be included? We're going to need all the help we can get. Salvatore isn't going to show up alone, if he shows up at all."

He gnashed his teeth together in frustration. The

last thing he wanted was for Kate to be put in the position of having to shoot anyone, even in self-defense. She'd followed through at the park, throwing the rock at the fake homeless guy, but shooting a person was far different.

That moment Jennifer had stood frozen still haunted him. In the split second she had had to make a life-and-death decision....

She'd died, because she couldn't do it.

In his mind, he could easily see Kate struggling the exact same way. Kate had faith, which meant she wouldn't be able to take a life easily. Not even in self-defense or to defend him.

And he didn't want her to have to make that choice. Especially not if she died, too, like Jennifer had.

"Do you have a floor plan of the building?" Nick asked, drawing Logan's attention from his dark thoughts.

"Yeah, on my laptop." He took a couple steps and brought the sleeping machine to life with the click of a button.

"We need to figure out where to have the transaction take place," Nick murmured as he peered at the blueprint.

"I planted the bug here," he said, lightly tapping the computer screen. "I thought that if Salvatore was going to talk anywhere it might be in this conference room."

"How much of the racetrack does Salvatore own?" Nick asked.

"Not quite half, with the money I gave him as part of my Tex Ryan cover," he admitted grimly. "I was supposed to make another deposit to get him to the 51 percent mark."

Nick raised a brow. "So you were a silent partner?"

He nodded. "With a chance to double my investment, and to have a place to race my prize Thoroughbred, Running Free."

Nick whistled under his breath. "Do you really have a racehorse?" When Logan nodded, the detective looked impressed. "Okay, what happens now? Where does Salvatore come up with the rest of the money?"

"That's exactly what I'm hoping to find out." He glanced at his watch. "We need to get within range of the track to listen in."

Kate straightened in her seat. "I'm coming with you," she announced.

He didn't see a way around it, so he reluctantly agreed. "All right, let's go."

He hoped and prayed that they would get something useful from their midnight breaking-and-entering caper to plant the bug.

Otherwise they'd be flying blind the day of the grand opening. Which wasn't at all reassuring, considering how the notorious crime boss already had the deck stacked against them.

Seated inside Nick Butler's car behind darkly tinted windows while parked a few blocks from Berkshire Racetrack, Logan fit the earpiece to his ear and turned up the receiver. Instantly, he could hear people talking from inside the main building. But it was difficult to figure out which voice belonged to which person. And from the jumble of voices, it sounded as if they were picking up conversations from outside the conference room.

Both Kate and Nick had earpieces, too, so that hopefully, between the three of them, they wouldn't miss anything important. Sitting around and doing nothing more than listening was tediously frustrating, but necessary if their plan was to succeed. He concentrated on trying to pick out either Salvatore's voice or Russo's from the crowd.

They all had notebooks so they could jot down anything they overheard that might be significant. From the corner of his eye, he noticed Kate was writing almost nonstop, which made him wonder if he was missing something.

At least Butler wasn't taking any notes yet, either, so Logan figured he must not be too much of a slacker. Or was Kate determined to write down everything in an attempt to put together the puzzle pieces later? He had to admire her dedication.

The hours passed slowly. Until a deep, raspy voice with a heavy Sicilian accent caught his attention.

"Is the place clean?" There was another noise that sounded like a door closing, before there was an answer from another man with a similar accent.

"Yes, it's clean."

He smiled with grim satisfaction that Salvatore was actually using the conference room as he'd predicted, and that Salvatore's bug sweep hadn't found their high-tech device.

"Good. Do we have him yet?"

"No. Unfortunately, he escaped, doing far more damage than expected."

Logan's breath froze in his lungs as he recognized both Russo's and Salvatore's voices. He wrote down exactly what was said, figuring they had to be talking about the park incident with the fake homeless guy. Although without proof, it was his word against theirs. Especially when the two mafia men were masters at not giving anything away that could be used against them.

"Does our source have a new location for him yet?"

"He claims he's working on it."

Who? Logan wanted to shout. *Who's the source?* He didn't want to believe it was anyone within the FBI task force, but the way it sounded, that was a distinct possibility. Obviously he and Kate had been followed at least once.

"If he doesn't produce results soon, we may have to replace him with someone better connected." The familiar edge to the tone convinced Logan the voice belonged to Salvatore. *"This has already gone on too long. We should have had him seventy-two hours ago. We can't afford any loose ends."*

"I agree. We need to get him and the woman before the opening. Which reminds me, did you get a commitment for the additional funding?"

Logan tensed at the reference to Kate. He'd hoped they were only after him, but apparently Kate was also a target. *Give me a name,* he silently begged. Something they could use as a potential starting point.

"Yes, the congressman came through. We have what we need and a little extra."

A little extra? He couldn't help but smile. Good to know. With money to spare, he was more convinced than ever that Salvatore would bite on buying the high-tech listening device. Especially since Salvatore wouldn't be able to resist the chance to get close to Logan.

"Call me if you hear from our source."

"Of course."

Moments later, there was the sound of a door opening, and more voices in the background filtered through, making his head hurt with the effort of trying to sort out anything. With a wry grimace, he tugged the device out of his ear and tossed it down.

"They didn't give us much," he muttered in disgust.

"Did you really think they would?" Nick asked mildly. "They haven't stayed in the organized crime business for this long without knowing how to keep their mouths shut. Even if they don't think that anyone can overhear them."

"I know," he said with a sigh. He glanced at Kate, who was still listening intently and taking notes. He wanted to tell her not to bother, but knew she wouldn't take any criticism from him very well. Since what she was doing was harmless, he turned back to Nick. "Which congressman do you think is dirty?"

"Very good question," Nick murmured. "I think we should head back to the motel to search for possible candidates."

He glanced at Kate, who'd finally taken out her earpiece. "Do you still think it's a good idea to contact Salvatore?" she asked. "He's obviously looking for you. That whole bit about you escaping and causing damage had to be related to the incident near the statue."

"Yeah, but did they say enough for us to prove it? Not even close."

"No, but isn't it enough that he threatened you?"

He stared at her for a long moment, wishing things could be different. But he wasn't ready to risk his heart again. And even if he were, the last thing he wanted was a relationship with another cop, whether she was one now or later.

A teacher, a nurse, a doctor, even a lawyer would be preferable to someone within the field of law enforcement. No matter how much he cared for Kate, he just didn't think he could go through that again.

Not after losing Jennifer.

Since she was still staring at him, with a mixture of hope and despair shining from her Irish-mud eyes, he forced himself to answer. "Don't worry, I'll be careful."

She set her jaw and hunched her shoulders as she turned away. He wanted to reach out and put his arm around her, to reassure her that everything would work out fine, but he stayed where he was.

Because he couldn't offer false promises.

And because it was better to distance himself from her now, before the attraction shimmering between them interfered with getting the job done.

For the next twenty-four hours, Kate's anger and frustration simmered beneath the surface. Logan and Nick spent hours either listening to what was going on inside the racetrack or searching out various Illinois congressmen, in an attempt to figure out the identity of Salvatore's newest financial partner.

The two men probably thought she was crazy to take so many notes, but there was a conversation in the background that had caught her attention. She wasn't able to get everything down, especially once the two Sicilians shut the door, but that didn't stop her from poring over her notes, trying to make sense of the snatches of words she'd captured on paper.

But time was running out. They had less than twenty-four hours before the grand opening and she knew Logan fully intended to contact Salvatore after the race.

He must have sensed her thoughts because he tapped on the connecting door between their rooms. "Butler is heading out to pick up supplies—do you want to come along?"

She glanced up from her notebook, searching his gaze. In the few days since Butler had joined their team, Logan had drifted further and further away. At times like this, she couldn't imagine he'd ever held her in his arms or kissed her. And she was surprised at how badly she wanted to turn back the clock, to recapture those stolen moments. "What kind of supplies?"

"Body armor, for one thing. Clothes to help us blend in during the grand opening."

She wrinkled her nose, knowing she probably

needed a dress. Although there was a discount store across the street that she'd thought would work well enough. As much as she wanted to be a part of the team, there was no point in tagging along. "No, I'll stay here for now. But do you mind if I borrow your computer while you're gone?"

His eyebrows shot up in surprise, but he shook his head. "Of course not. Help yourself."

"All right." She forced a smile, although she wanted very badly to ask Logan what she'd done to make him pull away from her. "I'll see you guys later, then."

"Sure." Logan turned, hesitated, as if he wanted to say something more, but instead he left the connecting door open, and walked away.

Her heart squeezed painfully, and she waited for several minutes after she heard the door shut behind them before she went over to boot up Logan's laptop.

Glancing at her notes again, she did a search on a few of the phrases she'd written down. She managed to get a hit on the third one.

She stared at the computer screen in shocked surprise. Chicago's Best was actually the name of a racehorse. A filly sired by the recent winner at the Churchill Downs Racetrack. When she glanced back at her notes, the seemingly nonsensical sentences suddenly became crystal clear.

THIRTEEN

Kate continued searching the internet for information.

She could hardly wait to show Logan the connection she'd discovered. They were starting to put together the puzzle pieces, but time was running out. They needed to be able to draw Salvatore away from his thugs, another long shot at best, in order to put the mobster behind bars once and for all.

While rubbing the fatigue from her eyes, a loud noise startled her so badly she fell off her chair, managing to catch herself just before she hit the floor.

"Are you all right?" Logan asked, rushing over to her side. He steadied her with his arm, and she felt the warmth of his touch all the way down to her toes.

She was hyperaware of his closeness and wished she wasn't, as her cheeks burned with embarrassment. "I'm fine. I guess I wasn't expecting you to be back so soon."

"Didn't take long to get what we needed," he murmured, glancing at her quizzically, as if trying to gauge her mood.

"Great." She tried to inject cheerfulness into her tone. "Look what I discovered while you were gone." She tapped the computer screen. "I took notes from the bits and pieces of a conversation I could hear going on behind Salvatore and Russo. See here? Chicago's Best is actually the name of a racehorse. And guess who owns her? Congressman George Stayman."

"Congressman Stayman," Logan echoed, leaning over her shoulder to read the article she'd found on the computer. "He must be Salvatore's silent partner."

"That's what I think, too," she agreed. "Plus his district includes the racetrack. And from what I gathered, it almost seems like the race is being fixed. According to this article, Chicago's Best is the least likely to win, at twenty-six-to-one odds. Yet what I overheard was that Chicago's Best was a sure thing based on an inside tip."

"Why am I not surprised?" Nick asked with a hint of sarcasm. "If that's true, I can see why the congressman put up the rest of the money for the track. He'll get his return on his investment almost immediately, along with the opportunity to win lots more."

"A perfect partnership, as this also gives Salvatore a way to launder his dirty money," Logan added grimly. He stared at the article for a long moment. "Too bad we can't prove it."

"Maybe we should go to the press?" she said, causing both men to turn to stare at her in surprise. "Why do you look so shocked? Any investigative reporter would love to dig into this allegation."

"Not a good idea. We can't afford to let Salvatore know before the race," Logan said. "Although maybe later, if our plan doesn't work, we could reconsider that option."

She wanted to remind him that using himself as bait was hardly a plan, but she held back with an effort. "A good investigative reporter wouldn't tip off Salvatore, and maybe having someone else watching the guy on race day would work in our favor."

"She has a point, Logan," Nick pointed out calmly.

She wanted to hug Nick for sticking up for her. "An investigative reporter would be more interested in the story than double-crossing us."

But Logan was shaking his head. "No way. We're not dragging anyone else into this mess. We'll only do that as a last resort."

Kate wanted to argue, but the stubborn set of his jaw told her that she'd only be wasting her breath. Logan might be strong, smart and caring, but when he decided something, he could be more stubborn than a mule.

And she was very much afraid that his stubbornness would be his downfall, if he insisted on contacting Salvatore and putting his life on the line in an attempt to set up the guy.

Logan could tell Kate was upset with him, but he refused to back down. Didn't she understand that he could handle just about anything except for losing her? He needed for her to stay safe more than he needed to breathe.

"What in the world did you buy?" she asked when Nick dumped out their bags on the table.

"A disguise for you to wear tomorrow," Nick teased. "Big floppy hat, bottle of hair dye and a long sundress."

"Hair dye?" she echoed with a grimace. "Yuck."

"It's temporary dye," Nick reassured her.

"Or you can stay here at the hotel where you'll be safe, and then you wouldn't need the hair dye," Logan couldn't help interjecting. "No reason for you to put your life on the line."

"Reddish-blond, huh?" she said, ignoring him. The smile she flashed at Nick was dazzling. "Great! I've always wanted to be a redhead."

Logan scowled, trying to rein in his temper. He didn't want Kate to be a redhead. He didn't want her to be at the racetrack, backing him up. He especially didn't want her anywhere near when he met with Salvatore, but Nick overrode every single one of his objections, telling him that they needed all the help they could get.

Which was probably true. But he didn't care. It was only because he wanted Nick to be safe, too, that he went along with the detective's plan.

"Do you both have disguises?" she asked, dragging his attention away from his dark thoughts.

"Yeah, although nothing dramatic," Nick said. "Dark glasses, baggy clothes—that type of thing."

"I need Salvatore to recognize me when we're ready to make our move," Logan spoke up.

He could tell her lips tightened, but she didn't say anything more. She picked up the hair dye and the clothes and headed toward the connecting doors between the rooms.

She shut the door and then locked it, making him wince. "She's not happy," he murmured.

"Look, buddy, far be it for me to pry into your business, but I think you're a little too anxious for this showdown with Salvatore. I'm getting the impression you don't care if he kills you, as long as you take him down with you."

Logan couldn't deny the thought had occurred to him. The world would be a far better place without the likes of Bernardo Salvatore. "I'm fine," he said tersely. "I don't have a death wish. I just want to put Salvatore behind bars before he kills anyone else."

Nick lifted up his hands. "Hey, I know. I feel the same way. But you have a personal vendetta against the guy, and I'm concerned that you're allowing your emotions to overrule your brain."

He let out a sigh and rubbed the back of his neck. Since Nick was going along with his plan, he couldn't hold back the truth. "Okay, yeah, I can't deny having a personal vendetta against the guy. He's into everything illegal—drugs, prostitution, gambling—you name it and he's behind it."

"Drugs?" Nick's eyebrows levered up. "I didn't know about that."

"I started my law enforcement career in the DEA, and during a sting operation, me and my partner were planning to raid a known drug house. Based on our intel, the place was supposed to be empty, but when we arrived, a couple kids were doing a buy right in front of the place." Even without closing his eyes, he could see the scene playing out in front of him. "I went after the guy with the money and the druggie ran straight toward Jen. She had her weapon trained on him, but she didn't move. Didn't shoot. The kid actually looked stunned for a moment, but then he didn't hesitate to fire at her. I ran over but too late. She died in my arms."

Nick's dark eyes were full of compassion. "I'm

sorry, Logan. I can't imagine what you went through."

"And you know the worst of it? The house was rigged to blow, because Salvatore knew we were going to bust in and he didn't care how many people he killed as long as he continued making a profit. Going back to Jen saved my life. Several good DEA agents were killed that night, along with Jen. And Salvatore got off scot-free to open up a new drug shop someplace else."

"Don't worry, we'll get him," Nick said grimly.

"I know." Logan wasn't worried. Because he'd been working for the past two years on nailing Salvatore, and nothing was going to stop him now.

Nothing.

Kate sat in stunned shock, her back pressed against the connecting doors between their rooms. She'd had no idea that Salvatore had been directly responsible for the death of Logan's fiancée.

But now that she'd overheard Logan's story, his actions and decisions made perfect sense. This was the reason he'd volunteered to go undercover as Tex Ryan. This was the reason he'd made the switch from being in the DEA to working on the FBI task force against organized crime.

And this was the reason he'd never allow himself to fall in love.

She knew she shouldn't take it personally, but

there was so much to admire about Logan that it was difficult to ignore her feelings. She'd been so happy that he seemed to be renewing his faith. She'd assumed he'd accepted her for who she was. And thought for sure he was ready to move forward with his life.

Obviously, she was wrong. On all three counts.

Granted, he'd warned her about his past and had made his feelings about her chosen profession clear. But she hadn't listened.

She closed her eyes and rested her head back against the door. *Please, Lord, keep Logan safe. Give him strength and help him to understand revenge isn't justice. Amen.*

Several hours later, Kate ran her hands through her newly dyed hair, trying not to wince at the result. So much for reddish-blond. The strands were bright red.

Don't be vain, she reminded herself. What she looked like on the outside didn't matter. As long as she could assist with keeping Nick and Logan safe, she didn't care.

Her stomach rumbled painfully. Glancing at her watch, she realized the hour was well past dinnertime. Resolutely, she marched across the room, unlocked and opened her door.

Nick Butler glanced up from the computer. "Wow, is your hair red!"

"Yeah, I noticed." She frowned. "Where's Logan?"

"He just called to let me know he's on his way back, but was stopping to pick up a bucket of chicken."

Just the thought of fried chicken made her mouth water. "Where was he?"

"Listening to the bug. Picking up more info if possible." Nick's teeth flashed in a broad smile. "You impressed him when you figured out about the congressman's racehorse."

She shouldn't have been happy to have gained Logan's approval, but deep down, she was. "He went there alone?"

Nick shrugged. "I've been working another angle, and since we're running out of time, we split up. I discovered that Salvatore donated funds to Congressman Stayman's election fund two years ago. I'm getting the distinct feeling that the two of them have been in cahoots for a while."

She dropped into the chair next to him. "First a state senator, and now a congressman? No wonder the public doesn't trust politicians."

"All it takes are a few bad apples," Nick agreed. When the distinct sound of the SUV pulled up, he stood and crossed over to the door.

Moments later, Logan strode in carrying a bucket of fried chicken, a tub of mashed potatoes and several bottles of water. He was also wearing a black cowboy hat and cowboy boots.

That was his disguise?

"Did you get anything?" Nick asked as he helped to unpack the food.

"Unfortunately not," Logan said, handing out paper plates and napkins. He swept his cowboy hat off his head and ran his fingers over his close-cropped hair. "The place was quiet, which surprised me. I figured the night before the opening day would be busy."

"Tomorrow morning might be busy," Nick mused, moving the computer and pulling up a third chair.

"We can only hope so." Logan sat next to Kate and then paused, looking over at her expectantly.

Despite her annoyance with him, her lips twitched. "Are you waiting for something?"

He looked startled. "Aren't you going to pray?"

"I think it's your turn." She put her hands together and bowed her head. She could feel Nick staring at them, as if trying to figure out if they were serious or not.

Logan hesitated a moment and then began. "Dear Lord, thank You for this food we are about to eat. Please keep us all safe from harm tomorrow. Amen."

"Amen," she echoed, pleased that he'd prayed out loud. "Thank you, Logan, for doing the honors."

"I'm just glad you included yourself in the part where you asked God to keep us safe from harm,"

Nick teased. He picked up a drumstick and took a huge bite. "Mmm, this hits the spot."

She took a thigh and silently agreed. Maybe Logan's faith would help him to realize that he had a lot to live for.

Even if he chose to leave her once they'd arrested Salvatore.

Kate slept better than she'd expected, and the next morning, she found herself anxious to get going. They packed up the SUV and checked out of the motel right at eleven o'clock.

She'd be thrilled if she never had to stay in a dive motel again.

Wearing the long gauzy dress and the wide-brimmed floppy hat felt weird, and she'd been forced to run over to the outlet store right before they left, to get a pair of flat shoes to wear with the dress, as the typical men hadn't thought about her footwear.

The dress was a bit impractical if she had to run, but at least the pockets were deep enough for her to hide a gun. Logan hadn't wanted her to carry one, but Nick had insisted that she be able to defend herself.

The weapon felt heavy, and for a moment she considered giving it back. She could shoot. Her father and her brothers had often taken her to the driving range, but she wasn't a cop yet and despite having permit to carry, she'd never walked around with a concealed weapon.

Yet the thought of being helpless if she needed to back up Logan was too much to bear. She'd rather step out of her comfort zone than risk losing him.

Logan pulled over to the side of the road, about a half mile from the Berkshire Racetrack. "We need to split up."

"I'll walk in from here," Nick volunteered. "You and Kate can go in together, and then from there you can spread out. The first race isn't scheduled until two o'clock this afternoon."

"All right." Logan waited until Nick jumped out of the SUV before glancing at her. "Are you ready?"

"Of course. Let's go."

They drove the rest of the way in and parked. The lot was full, with tons of people milling around, and she realized that the disguises were likely over-kill. Who was going to be able to find and recognize them amid this mass of people?

They strolled inside holding hands as if they were any other couple here to enjoy the day. Although in her mind, Logan was far more noticeable wearing his cowboy hat and cowboy boots, yet to be truthful he wasn't the only one. The clank and whirl of slot machines could be heard the instant the doors closed behind them, and she wrinkled her nose at the cloying scents of perfume mixed with aftershave. The building was broken into two main sections: to the left was a small casino area with slot machines and only about a half-dozen blackjack tables, whereas the area to the right was indoor seating and wide windows overlooking the racetrack. Straight ahead was a snack bar area, and right next to that were the lines for people to place their bets on the horses.

They meandered over to the snack bar, where there were hot dogs and hamburgers for sale. Logan ordered a quick lunch, paying an outrageous amount of money for the basic fare.

Kate swept her gaze over the crowd and caught her breath when she thought she saw a familiar face.

Garrett? Was that really her brother she'd seen ducking into the casino area?

"I'll be right back," she said, leaving her half-finished chicken sandwich and cutting through the crowd. She stood in the doorway and scanned the people playing slots and blackjack, but didn't find him.

As she made her way back to Logan, she tried to tell herself that maybe she had let her imagination get away from her. Garrett wouldn't be here at the racetrack or the casino.

Unless he thought he could help by keeping tabs on Salvatore?

When she reached Logan's side, he clamped his

hand around her wrist. He leaned close, putting his mouth right by her ear. "Glance over to your right," he said tersely.

Moving slowly, she did as he asked. For a moment she didn't know who he was talking about, and then she saw him.

Congressman George Stayman. Looking older and at least twenty pounds heavier than his photograph she'd seen online. "I see him," she whispered.

"Keep your eyes sharp," Logan said softly. "I'm sure Salvatore will be here soon."

She nodded, trying not to stare at the congressman, who was surrounded by a mini-entourage of people. When a woman with particularly heavy perfume came up beside her, she sneezed several times in a row. For whatever reason, she hadn't expected the place to be so crowded.

"I'm going to follow him for a bit," Logan murmured. "Are you going to be okay?"

She nodded, not afraid of something bad happening within the crowd surrounding her. Before Logan could move, the doors opened and her heart squeezed in her chest.

Salvatore and Russo! She gripped the back of Logan's shirt to stop him from leaving. He stiffened as he caught sight of them, too. The two men were unmistakable and just happened to be surrounded by several other men who were no doubt thugs paid to protect them.

Salvatore crossed the room, jovially greeting the congressman. From the other side of the room she caught sight of Nick Butler, and it took her a moment to realize he was subtly taking a picture of the two men shaking hands. They spoke for a moment before turning away, heading through a set of doors to the private office area.

The conference room! Logan must have had the same thought, because he moved swiftly through the crowd, intent on getting back outside to the SUV and the equipment they'd stored there.

She stayed where she was, sipping her water as if she didn't have a care in the world. She saw Nick Butler again, but didn't make eye contact. She continued to scan the crowd, hoping to catch a glimpse of the man who resembled her brother.

If Garrett was here out of some misguided idea of helping her, she needed to warn him to stay away. The last thing she wanted was for her brother to get hurt in the midst of taking down Salvatore.

So where was he?

Logan lengthened his stride to get to the SUV as quickly as possible. He wanted to hear the conversation going on in that room.

He reached the car, and yanked open the door.

He fit the earpiece inside his ear and immediately heard voices.

"It's clean?"

"Yes, this place is secure. My men swept for bugs."

Logan smiled grimly.

"Is everything all set?"

"Yes. Did you doubt my ability?"

"No, of course not." Logan identified the speaker as the congressman, and when he laughed, Logan sensed a hint of nervousness. *"You know I'm grateful for our alliance."*

"And our mutually beneficial alliance will continue, as long as you hold up your end of the bargain."

Logan was glad to have this conversation recorded. The first step of proving the congressman and Salvatore were in business together.

"Here you go, five hundred Gs. I always pay my debts."

"Debts?" Salvatore let out a humorless laugh. *"My dear congressman, this is only the beginning."*

There was a long pause, leaving Logan to imagine the scene in the conference room. Clearly, Salvatore was planning to use his connections with the congressman in the future, and he wasn't sure the congressman was thrilled with the idea. Something he should have considered before creating an alliance with a snake like Salvatore.

"The beginning of this racino making us both rich."

"I certainly hope so. Now, there's less than an hour before the start of the race. If you want to place your bets, better do so before the windows close."

"I plan on it. And I'll see you in the winner's circle."

Logan ripped out the earpiece and shut off the recorder. For the first time in a week, he felt they were getting close. There was no mistaking the intent during this conversation, and while he was somewhat surprised that the congressman and Salvatore had gotten together on race day, he knew they were both arrogant enough to believe they could get away with anything.

Even murder.

FOURTEEN

Logan headed back inside the building, settling the cowboy hat firmly on his head as adrenaline surged in his veins. They had the first part of the plan nailed. They had proof that Salvatore and Congressman Stayman were in cahoots together.

It was almost time to put the second part of the plan in motion. The part where he made contact with Salvatore and convinced the mobster that he was in trouble with the FBI and wanted to sell off the high-tech listening device.

But first, they had to watch the race, which was obviously fixed so that Chicago's Best would win.

He found Kate chatting with an elderly couple, and tried not to wince at her attempt to talk with a Southern accent. "Why, here's my husband now. Tex, I'd like you to meet Sharon and Clive Erringer. They've come all the way up here from Kentucky!"

"Do y'all have a horse in the race?" Logan asked, as he slipped an arm around Kate's waist. He gave her a warning squeeze, not at all happy that she'd referred to him as Tex Ryan. And that she was playing the role of his wife. What in the world was she thinking? The Tex Ryan cover was blown. Although he'd only used it when dealing with Salvatore and his men.

"Why, yes, as a matter of fact we do," the elder gentleman said with a broad smile. "We have a two-year-old colt in the race, Jacob's Pride."

He searched his memory; his brother and his father, who ran the Lazy Q ranch, often talked about various racehorses. They'd trained several Thoroughbreds. "Wasn't Jacob's Run his sire?"

Clive Erringer let out a loud bellow of a laugh. "Yes, indeed he was. Great horse, won several major races back six or seven years ago. We have high hopes for his colt. He's favored to place in the top three, if you're interested in placing a bet."

"I'm not a betting man, but I still like the excitement of a good race." It bothered Logan that this nice couple was about to be a victim of Salvatore's scam, but there was nothing he could do right now to salvage the race. Although now that he thought about it, he wasn't sure exactly how the congressman and Salvatore would sabotage the other horses that would be running their hearts out, like Jacob's Pride. Did they have someone working inside the stables? Would they slip the horses some sort of drug that might slow them down? Didn't vets take blood samples of the horses? Probably not in a lower race like this one. It wasn't as if Berkshire Racetrack was on the same level as the big three, the Preakness, the Derby and the Belmont.

Either way, he figured it wouldn't be easy to fix a race, since most owners were pretty protective of their racehorses, to the point of serving all food and water themselves from only trusted sources. But those details were something to figure out later.

Tonight, all he could do was to follow their plan, as loose as it was, to make sure that Salvatore paid for his crimes.

Kate followed the Erringers outside, putting a hand up to prevent the floppy hat from flying off her head in the wind. The excitement in the air was tangible, hundreds of people anxious to partake in the first race of the newest racetrack.

Although she noticed that several stayed in the casino portion of the building where televisions had been mounted in strategic locations for casino players to keep an eye on the race. Obviously they weren't about to give up their spot at the blackjack table or at a hot slot machine to watch the two-and-a-half-minute race.

The crowded casino helped her understand why the congressman had worked so hard to make sure that the racino bill went through. The racetrack itself wasn't where he and Salvatore would make the bulk of their money.

Not only would the casino bring in cash, but it was a good place to launder dirty money. She shook her head at the casino players' foolishness. Gambling was a waste of time and money.

She stood next to Logan, watching as the race handlers helped line up the horses and their respective jockeys in the gate. One horse balked at going in, fighting its rider by rearing his head back and prancing sideways. After a few minutes the jockey managed to control the horse long enough to get him into the gate.

"Jacob's Pride is number seven," Sharon confided. "Lucky number seven and our colors are red and gold."

Kate smiled and nodded, even though she was feeling sorry for the horses. Injuries were not uncommon, and no matter how often Clive and Sharon tried to say that the colt loved to run, Kate felt for the endangered horses. Soon, the last gate was filled and there was just a brief moment before the bell sounded and the gates flew open to start the race. She caught her breath at the sight of the racehorses flying out across the track. Kate found herself gripping the railing tightly as the horses crowded together along the turn.

Clive and Sharon were yelling at the top of their lungs, screaming for Jacob's Pride. There were immediately several front-runners, including Jacob's Pride and Chicago's Best. She reverently hoped that

Salvatore hadn't figured out a way to fix the race, as Chicago's Best lagged behind in fourth place.

But as the horses rounded the last turn and headed down the home stretch, she could see Chicago's Best inching up the middle between Jacob's Pride and Freedom Rings. Her fingers tightened on the railing as Chicago's Best gave one last surge, winning the race by a nose, followed by Jacob's Pride in second place and Freedom Rings in third.

For a moment she could only stare in shock, as the winning horse pranced around the track. If she hadn't overheard the comments about the race being fixed, she never would have suspected anything was amiss.

Certainly Clive and Sharon didn't suspect anything; they were cheering at the fact that Jacob's Pride had come in second place. "Did y'all see that?" Clive asked, thumping Logan on the back. "I told y'all that Jacob's Pride would place in the top three."

And probably would have won, if not for whatever Salvatore and Congressman Stayman had done to fix the race. If they really had. She couldn't help feeling some doubt. "Congratulations," Kate said warmly. "I'm so happy for you."

"That horse has a lot of heart, just like his daddy," Sharon murmured, giving her husband a hug. "And the way he ran today, he's going to do great."

"That he is," Clive agreed. "Nice meeting you both, but we're going to head down to check on the colt. Want to make sure he's all right."

"I understand. It was nice meeting y'all." Logan tipped his hat and moved over to the side, giving the older couple room to maneuver around them.

"What do you think?" she asked Logan in a low voice as soon as the older couple vanished through the crowd. "Was that race really fixed? And if so, how? I have to say from here it certainly looked real."

"Hard to know for sure, especially since it's not going to be easy to confirm how it was done. On the other hand, considering the horse had twenty-six-to-one odds, everyone who bet on him made a nice bundle of cash, so it's a bit suspect." His gaze swept over the crowd, searching for Salvatore, she was certain.

"He'll be watching the congressman accept his win," she guessed, gesturing down to where a crowd had gathered around the winner's circle. She could see the heavyset congressman smiling and shaking hands, accepting his congratulations with grace.

Regardless of the fact that he might not have earned it fairly.

"Maybe," he acknowledged. "But it's time for us to split up for a bit."

She didn't want to split up. She'd rather stay

glued to Logan's side. But now that the race was over, she knew he planned to make contact with Salvatore to make the offer of selling the listening device.

"Logan," she called as he moved away. He paused and turned back toward her. "Please be careful. Remember that you have a lot to live for. I'll pray for you, asking God to keep you safe."

He stared at her for a long moment, his gaze enigmatic. "I appreciate that," he finally murmured. "And I'll pray for you and Butler, too. We're going to get him, Kate. By the end of the night, this will be all over."

As he turned to weave his way through the crowd, she tried to be comforted by the fact that Logan didn't act like a man who was willing to recklessly endanger his life in the process of getting close to Salvatore. Determined, yes, but not reckless.

Full of hope, she did as she'd promised, sending up a quick, silent prayer to keep him safe.

Logan waited for what seemed like forever for the hubbub of the race to settle down before he decided to draw out Salvatore's attention. As the group around the winner's circle began to disperse, he made his move.

"Congressman Stayman!" he called. "Congrats on your win today."

"Thank you very much," he said, although his gaze narrowed as he stared at him, seemingly trying to figure out who he was. "Have we met?"

"We have a mutual friend, Bernardo Salvatore."

The congressman looked appalled for a fraction of a second before his expression cleared. "Mr. Salvatore has assisted with my campaign, but I don't know him well enough to call him a friend. Excuse me, but I have to check on my horse."

"Of course." Logan stepped back, thinking the congressman should have taken care to check on his horse much sooner. But he stayed where he was, scanning the crowd until he found Salvatore standing roughly fifty feet away near the top of the stands.

Their gazes clashed and held, and Logan couldn't help tipping his hat toward the mobster. Then he picked up his phone and dialed Salvatore's private number.

"You're a dead man, Tex Ryan," Salvatore growled into his ear. "I don't care who you work for, you're a dead man."

"Maybe. But before you try to kill me, you should know I have a high-tech bug that I think you'd be interested in owning for yourself."

There was a pause before Salvatore spoke. "I don't trust you and I don't believe you. A rather pathetic attempt on your part to set me up, don't you think?"

"Look, since your guy Russo busted me, my boss cut me loose. I'm hanging in the wind without backup. The only thing I have is a device that can't be picked up through a regular sweep. And I'd be happy to sell it to you, for a nice price."

"You're bluffing."

Logan began to move, weaving his way through the thinning crowd, since he wouldn't put it past Salvatore to kill him on sight. But he stayed on the phone. "No, I'm not. I heard every word of your conversation with the congressman. He paid you five hundred thousand dollars for his portion of the racetrack, and maybe a little more to cover the way you fixed the race. And I believe you said something about how this was the beginning of a mutually beneficial alliance."

"How do I know you haven't already gone to the Feds with this information?" Salvatore asked.

"I told you, they cut me loose. I need the money from this bug to leave the country. Why else would I be calling you with this offer?"

He expected Salvatore, or maybe Russo, to head straight for the conference room to look for the bug. Although by now, Nick Butler had already removed it. The detective had texted him a while ago and they'd agreed to bump into each other, to make the handoff with the device, since Logan needed it in order to convince Salvatore he was serious about selling it.

"All right, you have my attention," Salvatore finally said. "Name your price."

"One hundred thousand," he said. "After all, you received more than you needed from the congressman, didn't you?"

Salvatore muttered a string of phrases in his native tongue, something less than complimentary, he was sure. "Fine. But I will control the timing of the transaction."

Logan didn't have any illusions about Salvatore's intent. If there was a way for the mobster to kill him and get the listening device, he'd do it. "I'm not a fool, Salvatore. I can always find someone else to sell the device to. Meanwhile, the Feds will still have the technology, and I'm sure my former team won't hesitate to look for a way to use it against you."

Another stream of Sicilian curses burned his ear, and he was glad he didn't know exactly what was being said. Still, he waited for Salvatore to calm down. "What do you suggest?" Salvatore finally asked.

Logan smiled grimly. "I'll call you back in a couple of hours." Before Salvatore could protest, he disconnected from the call.

Next, he contacted Butler. "Salvatore is interested. Have you found a location for the transaction?"

"Yeah, I think so," Butler said. "There's a small

building toward the end of the barns, used to store tack and other supplies. It's far enough out of the way that, once the last race is over, we should be able to use it without being disturbed."

Logan could see only a corner of the building from where he was standing. He kept moving, trying to stay far away from Salvatore. "I think I see it. We'll have to make sure that it's empty. I don't want any innocent bystanders to get in the way."

"I hear you. The place will clear out pretty fast as the races end, although the casino portion of the building will be open until three in the morning. Let me take a look around, and I'll call you back."

Three in the morning. He didn't like it, but surely the die-hard gamblers wouldn't bother to wander down to the stables where the owners kept the horses. He knew from his father and brother that the owners liked to have the racehorses on site for up to a week before the race to help keep the animals calm. But he couldn't be sure how many of them would clear out as soon as the race was over.

Hopefully most, if not all.

Because he couldn't afford to fail in the third portion of the plan. The most dangerous part of all.

He moved into the casino area, where it was easier to get lost in the crowd, and tried to think of another place to use for the transaction. There might be something close by, but they didn't exactly have time to set up an elaborate plan. They were winging this on a hope and a prayer.

He'd have to trust Butler's judgment. And find a way to keep Kate well out of the way.

His phone rang again, about ten minutes later. It wasn't easy to hear over the din of the slot machines. "I had a conversation with a stable hand, and most of the horses are getting packed up right after the last race," Butler informed him. "I'd say we'll have most of the area around the stables to ourselves by early evening."

"All right. Is there cover nearby?"

"Not as much as I'd like," Butler said frankly. "We can probably place Kate in the empty horse stall next to the tack room, but she won't have a clear shot at covering you."

As long as Kate was safe, he didn't much care if she had a clear shot at covering him. He didn't want her anywhere near him once he confronted Salvatore. "All right, let's do it. But I don't want to give Salvatore time to set up a trap. We have to be ready to roll when I make the call."

"I hear you." Butler paused, and then asked, "Have you told Kate the plan?"

"Not yet." He was a little surprised he hadn't seen Kate since they parted ways. "Do you know where she is?"

There was a tense pause. "No. I thought she was with you."

Logan pinched the bridge of his nose and tried to breathe normally. There was no reason to panic. Kate had told him on more than one occasion that she could take care of herself.

He'd thought it would be safer for her to stay away from him while he made contact with Salvatore. Now he doubted the wisdom of his logic. He worked to keep his tone even. "We just split up about forty-five minutes ago. She can't be too far."

"We need to find her before Salvatore or Russo figure out who she is," Butler said in a tone full of grim determination.

A chill rippled down his spine, spreading cold fear through his entire body. What if Salvatore already had her? What if he wanted to make a trade for Kate's life?

Dear Lord, please keep Kate safe. Don't let Salvatore get his hands on her. Please?

He strove to remain calm. "I'll find her," he said. "You figure out the logistics of my meeting with Salvatore."

"All right, call me back as soon as you have Kate."

Logan ended the call and carefully looked around the casino portion of the racetrack. They hadn't replaced Kate's cell phone, so he couldn't simply call her. But surely she was here somewhere. As far as he could tell, every single blackjack table was full, as were most of the slot machines. He didn't see her brightly colored dress, her red hair or her floppy hat. He moved back toward the main area of the racetrack, but she wasn't there, either.

Was it possible she'd gone back to the SUV to get a change of clothes? They'd packed all their things from the hotel, and the jeans and sweatshirt would be more functional than the long dress.

But even so, she certainly didn't have time to dye her hair back to its normal color. So he concentrated on searching out the redheads.

But to no avail. Kate wasn't anywhere in the building, so he went back outside, first to the stands overlooking the racetrack, and then back through the building to head to the main entrance from the parking area.

He went as far into the parking lot as he dared. He didn't want to draw Salvatore's attention. Frustration mounting, he went inside.

He stood once again, in the back corner of the casino, racking his brain as he continued to scan the patrons.

Where on earth could Kate be?

FIFTEEN

Logan fought the rising sense of panic, even though he knew there was an entire area outside the racetrack building where Kate could be hiding. He was about to call Nick to ask him to search the stables when he noticed a redhead who wasn't Kate get up from her seat at the blackjack table and walk over to the ladies' room.

The one place where Kate could go without being followed by a man.

He inwardly rolled his eyes at his own foolishness for not thinking of that possibility earlier, but couldn't relax completely, not until he knew for sure that Kate was fine. He couldn't bear the thought of her being in danger from Salvatore.

He wandered closer to the door of the ladies' room, avoiding eye contact with the redheaded woman who wasn't Kate when she came out. He wanted to duck inside, but hesitated for fear of being seen and tossed out.

A short, rather heavyset woman with gray hair

approached the restroom. He stopped her, flashing his most charming smile. "Ma'am, my friend Kate is in the ladies' room and hasn't come out for a long time. I'm getting worried about her. Would you please check for me?"

"Of course, dear," the woman assured him. "What does your lady friend look like?"

"She's not very tall, about five feet four inches, slender with red hair." He avoided describing how Kate was dressed, in case she'd changed.

"I'll check on her," the older woman assured him, patting his arm as if he were her son. She disappeared inside and he waited tensely, hoping he wasn't wasting his time here if Kate needed him elsewhere.

Several long minutes later, Kate emerged from the ladies' room, dressed in the black jeans and black boots from their midnight breaking-and-entering run. A black baseball hat covered a good portion of her dyed red hair. He wanted to collapse against the wall with relief, even though she was scowling at him.

"What were you thinking, sending that lady in there to find me?" she asked in a low voice. "Talk about being obvious!"

"I needed to know you were safe," he murmured, unwilling to apologize for what he'd done. Because given the same set of circumstances, he knew he'd do it again. "Come on, let's get out of here."

"Did he take the bait?" she asked in a low voice as they edged through the casino. He kept Kate close to the wall, hiding her as much as possible from the people at the tables and slot machines. Once they reached the main area of the building, they ducked outside and walked around to the side of the building. The races were over and the crowd was thinning out.

There was a chill in the air as the sun had started to set, although not quickly enough to suit him. He'd prefer if it was pitch-black when they made the high-tech disk swap.

"Yeah. He's waiting for me to make the call," he informed her. He took out his phone, intending to call Butler, but she grabbed his arm.

"Wait! Let's talk this through first!" She looked horrified. "We need a solid plan."

He quickly realized Kate was afraid he was going to call Salvatore right now. "Relax, I'm just letting Nick know that I found you. We've both been a little worried."

"Oh." She dropped her hand and flushed as if embarrassed. "Go ahead then."

"Thanks," he said drily. He pushed the button to call Nick, and the detective answered almost immediately. "I found her."

"That's a relief. I brought the equipment from the SUV down to the tack room. A few horses are still being housed in the stable, but none close to the tack room."

The setup wasn't perfect, but it would have to do. From where they stood against the north side of the building, he had a clear view of the stables. "All right, we'll head down there before I call Salvatore."

"Okay, see you soon."

He disconnected the call and turned to Kate. "We're going to arrange the sale of the device down in the tack room at the end of the stable. There's an empty stall on the other side of the wall. I'm going to ask you to stay there."

Kate narrowed her gaze. "How am I going to back you up from there?"

He hesitated, knowing this was the tricky part. "I need you to listen in on the transaction. I'm going to get Salvatore to talk and I need you to record everything so that we can arrest him."

She stared at him as if he'd completely lost his mind. "That plan doesn't make any sense at all. Why would Salvatore talk to you? Especially when he knows you have the device? He isn't going to say anything when he knows we could be listening."

"I'm going to do my best," he said, knowing it wasn't exactly a reassuring answer. "I'm hoping to use the information I already know from the time I was undercover."

She slowly shook her head. "I don't like this, Logan. We don't have much leverage."

"We'll make it work," he assured her. But he refrained from adding that he'd do whatever possible to make that happen.

Including putting himself in God's hands to do as He willed.

Kate held back from unloading her frustration on Logan as they made their way to the stable. The grassy area between the main racetrack building and the stables was fairly open, with just a few strategically placed trees to provide some shade from the daytime sun.

But now, with dusk setting in, the trees helped to provide some coverage for the two of them, hopefully without being seen.

"Where do you think Salvatore is?" she asked as they reached the relative safety of the stable.

"I'm sure he's inside the conference room, plotting a way to get rid of us after we make the deal."

Great, and wasn't that a reassuring thought? Her scowl deepened as she tried to think of a way to improve on Logan's plan. There had to be some other way to spring this trap, one that didn't put Logan's life at risk.

"How do you know he doesn't have someone following us?" she asked.

He shrugged. "I don't know for sure. But I knew that he'd head back to the conference room to try to find the bug I'd originally planted there. Since he knows I have it now, the room is probably the most secure place for the moment."

"And you really think he'll come here to buy the device?"

"Yes, I do." Logan's clipped tone put an end to that line of conversation. He tapped on the door of a small building. "This is the tack room."

The door wasn't locked, and when they walked inside, there wasn't much light provided by the single bulb that hung down from the center of the ceiling. There were harnesses, stirrups and other gear lining the walls. On the one closest to the door there was a sawhorse with a saddle sitting on top of it.

Butler was standing behind the saddle, working on the wall with a small knife. "What do you think?" he asked, stepping aside. "Can you tell there's an opening here?"

"Not from back here," Logan drawled. "We'll have to make sure that Salvatore and his goons don't get too close."

"Let me see," she said, crossing over to where Butler stood. There was a natural knot in the wood that had a small hole in the center from where he'd drilled through with the knife.

"Is that going to be big enough?" she asked doubtfully.

"Has to be." Nick's expression was grim. "I made two openings, one for you to look through and another in case you need to use your weapon in self-defense. Go and see how they look from the other side."

"I'm calling Salvatore," Logan said, pulling out his cell phone.

Kate didn't waste another second, quickly leaving the tack room and going around to the empty horse stall, which unfortunately smelled too much like the wrong end of a horse. She wrinkled her nose and felt along the wall until she found the small opening. Thankfully, the hole was low enough for her to see through without crouching, and when she pressed her eye to the opening, gave her a surprisingly good view of the tack room.

Drawing back, she found the other small hole Nick had created, down and to the right, just large enough for her to shoot through if necessary. The angle probably wouldn't be enough to aim at a person, but she could cause a diversion. Down in the right-hand corner of the stall she saw the small receiver and tape recorder from the SUV, completely covered in hay. She could just barely make out the small green blinking light, and realized that Nick had somehow strung the wiring to tie into the light up in the ceiling.

Stepping back, she surveyed her surroundings. Not bad. If she hadn't been looking for it, she wouldn't have seen it. Although it wasn't a foolproof hiding spot, she felt a little better about the third phase of their plan.

She peered through the small opening, watching Logan's face as he made the call. "Do you still want the device or not?" She found herself holding her breath as he listened intently to whatever Salvatore was saying. "Meet me in the tack room at the end of the stables in fifteen minutes," he said. "Don't bring anyone else except Russo and make sure you bring the cash."

Salvatore must have agreed, because Logan hung up the phone and glanced at his watch. "We have five minutes at the most. I figure it will take at least that long for them to get down here."

She pulled out the small gun Nick had given her from the small of her back, but the palms of her hands went damp with nerves. She swiped them on the sides of her jeans, taking a slow deep breath to steady herself. She lined up the barrel of the gun against the small opening, and then pressed her eye against the part of the wall where the knot in the wood would be. "I'm okay on this side," she said in a low voice.

The two men glanced at the wall and nodded. "Make sure the recorder is on," Logan said.

"I'll be outside," Nick said, heading for the door. "Unless you've changed your mind? You know Salvatore will come down with more backup than just Russo."

A rueful grin tugged at the corner of Logan's mouth. "That's why I need you outside. I'm counting on you to help even the odds out there."

"Don't worry, I'm on it." Butler disappeared before she could blink.

Kate closed her eyes for a moment, the bitter taste of fear coating her mouth. What were they thinking? Three good guys against how many bad guys?

They should have called Logan's boss again. Or a few cops Nick trusted. Or her brothers. Anyone who could help even the odds that seemed to be stacked so steeply against them.

She remembered that night six months ago, when she and Logan had helped Mallory Roth and Jonah Stewart to escape the Milwaukee police chief who'd trapped them in an old abandoned warehouse that had been rigged to explode. The odds hadn't been in their favor back then, either, and somehow they'd managed to escape.

She could only pray that they'd do the same this time.

Please, Lord. Please keep Nick and Logan safe. Provide us the strength and wisdom to stop Salvatore. Let Your will be done. Amen.

Within two minutes Kate could hear the sounds of footsteps outside the tack room door. Logan stood in the center of the room, waiting, looking as relaxed as she was tense. She jumped when the door burst open.

"You're a bit early, Salvatore," Logan greeted the mobster. Although she noted that Russo was the one who stepped inside first, putting his life on the line in order to protect his boss. Both men were armed, their guns trained directly on Logan.

Salvatore bared his teeth in what she assumed was his attempt at a smile. "Why would I give you more of an advantage than you already have?"

"I don't have the advantage," Logan protested, holding up his hands to show he wasn't armed. "You two have your guns pointed directly at me. All I have is the device. Thanks to your goon Russo, I lost everything."

From her vantage point, she could see Russo was walking the perimeter of the room, as if assuring that no one was hiding there. He didn't look close enough to see the holes Nick had made in the wall. And she hoped Russo wouldn't go so far as to come around to search the stall where she was hiding.

"I believe it was your own weakness in choosing to save the woman that caused you to lose everything," Salvatore countered. "And for what? Where is she now?"

"I let her go. She's not a part of this. Isn't it enough that you have the congressman on your payroll? Makes me wonder why you bothered to try and get money from Tex Ryan in the first place."

"Obviously, I was hoping to get a piece of your oil wells," Salvatore admitted. "However, since you're not Tex Ryan, I'm assuming there are no oil wells, which doesn't make me happy. It's a good thing I always have a backup plan."

The tiny hairs on her neck tingled in warning, and she tightened her grip on the gun, trying to line up the angle of the hole in the wall with the two armed men standing in the room.

She recognized a veiled threat when she heard one. Were they going to kill Logan right in front of her eyes? If that was their intent, she would be helpless to stop them. Granted she could return fire, but the chance of her actually hitting either man was slim to none.

"I hate to admit, I admire your cunning," Logan drawled. "What did you and Russo want with the blonde anyway? I can't believe that slip of a girl posed a serious threat to your vast organization."

"She had information I wanted. However, we managed to work around it. As it turned out, you showed your true colors for nothing." Salvatore was obviously trying to get under Logan's skin.

"Maybe, but the way you blew up Burke Townsend's safe to destroy the evidence he'd gathered against you wasn't exactly subtle," Logan said calmly. "All you managed to do was to draw attention to yourselves."

"Aah, so you do know the identity of the woman

you saved." Salvatore took a step forward, but Logan stayed where he was. "I can see the two of you were obviously working together. So where is she now?"

Fear caused her heart to pound so loud, she could barely hear Salvatore's low voice. So far, the mobster hadn't said anything terribly incriminating. Other than pointing their weapons at Logan with the intent to get the listening device.

Would that be enough to arrest him? To convict him?

Even if they managed to get out of this alive?

She doubted it.

"I left her days ago," Logan said. "She doesn't deserve any part of the cash you're about to pay me."

"You really think I'm going to pay you?" Salvatore asked. "Why wouldn't I simply shoot you now?"

"Because the device is encrypted with a code." Logan held up the nickel-sized disk for both Russo and Salvatore to see. "Did you think I'd be so foolish as to meet you here without some sort of ace in the hole? Here's how this is going to work. You pay me, and I give you the disk. Once I'm safe, I'll call to give you the code."

Salvatore and Russo hesitated for a moment, glancing at each other as if to judge whether or not to believe him. That fraction of a second was all they needed.

Logan rushed Salvatore, who was the closest to him, at the exact same instant that Nick Butler kicked open the door, aiming his gun directly at Russo.

Instinctively, she squeezed the trigger of her own weapon aimed as close to Russo as she could get. She didn't hit him, but the sound of gunfire coming from the wall behind him was enough to distract his attention from Nick.

Nick shot Russo, while Salvatore and Logan wrestled on the floor for Salvatore's gun. Russo staggered backward, clutching his wounded right shoulder as blood streamed down his arm. But he didn't let go of his weapon, gripped in his right hand.

"Drop the gun!" Butler shouted.

Russo brought up his injured right arm, intending to shoot, but too late. Butler shot again, this time hitting Russo in the chest.

Kate wrenched herself away from the wall and ran into the tack room. By the time she arrived, Nick and Logan were tying up an unconscious Salvatore.

For a moment she could only stand there in shock. "Is there anyone else outside?" she asked, afraid to believe it was really over.

"Russo and Salvatore brought two other thugs with them, but me and my buddy took them out," Butler assured her. "Jake Andrews is one of the few cops I trusted implicitly, and he's already hustled the two of them out of here."

She dragged her gaze away from Logan, who was tightening the harness he'd used to tie up Salvatore, to look over at where Russo had fallen to the ground. She tucked her gun into the waistband of her jeans at the small of her back and walked forward. She was fairly certain the thug was dead, but she forced herself to make sure.

His skin was still warm, but there was no pulse. Russo was dead.

"I didn't have a choice," Nick said grimly, coming up beside her. "He didn't drop his weapon."

"I know." She didn't understand why she was so upset. This was the same man who'd held her at gunpoint, threatening to kill her if she didn't talk. She knew that Butler's first shot had been an attempt to disarm him, and the thug had the opportunity to toss down his weapon.

But no matter what she knew logically—that Nick Butler didn't have a choice but to kill him—she still felt sick.

"At least it's over," she murmured. "I only hope we have enough evidence to put away Salvatore for a long time."

"We will."

"Don't move," a deep voice said loudly, interrupting them.

She spun around to find her older brother Garrett standing next to Logan. For a moment, she didn't understand, because her brother had his arm locked around Logan's neck, holding the tip of his gun firmly against the side of Logan's temple.

"What are you doing?" she asked.

"Drop your weapons and stay right where you are," Garrett said harshly. "Don't make me kill him."

Kill him? She stared in shock, unable to wrap her mind around the scene unfolding in front of her. None of this made any sense. Why would Garrett hold Logan at gunpoint? Did he think she was still in some sort of danger? She heard a thud as Nick dropped his gun.

"Take one step slowly backward," her brother said to Logan. She met Logan's gaze as he obliged Garrett by doing so, bringing the two men closer to the door.

"Garrett, stop it," she pleaded. "Don't you understand? Logan works for the FBI!"

"Shut up!" Garrett shouted. "You weren't supposed to be here. Why didn't you listen to me, Katie? Why?"

His words slowly sank into her brain, and her stomach clenched painfully as she realized the truth.

Her brother Garrett was one of the dirty cops working for Salvatore. And he was acting like a desperate man with nothing to lose.

SIXTEEN

Waves of anger and despair battered her with the unrelenting force of a tsunami. How she stayed on her feet, she never knew. She desperately tried to pull herself together, as if her life as she knew it weren't disintegrating before her eyes. She sensed Nick stepping closer to her as if trying to offer support, but she ignored him.

She couldn't tear her eyes from her brother Garrett. His blond hair and Irish-mud eyes, both so similar to her own. She recalled his strength, especially the way he'd given her a shoulder to cry upon when she was younger.

The brother who'd sat beside her in church, week after week, along with the rest of the family.

A rising denial threatened to choke her. How had this happened? When? Why? So many questions without time for answers.

Dear God, help me! Save Logan! And save Garrett, too. Please, Lord, please don't abandon us now.

The prayer helped her to gather some semblance of control. "Don't do this, Garrett," she pleaded. "I'll help you. I promise I'll help you if you stop right now."

"You can't help me," Garrett said harshly, his face grim. "Only Salvatore can. I want you and that cop friend of yours to stand back against the wall."

She gaped at him, her feet glued to the floor.

"Do it!" he shouted.

She forced herself to move, taking a tentative step backward, as did Nick. She couldn't bear to look at Logan, not wanting to see the censure in his eyes. She couldn't imagine how he felt right now, being held at gunpoint by her brother. *Her brother!* A situation that was all her fault.

Somehow she had to save them both. Because if either Logan or Garrett died tonight, she'd never recover.

"Garrett, please listen to me," she begged. "You can see we have Salvatore tied up, we'll turn him over to the FBI. He can't hurt you from prison." Or could he? Her stomach twisted painfully, and she tried not to consider the possibilities. "What is it you need? Money?" She remembered how she'd thought she'd seen Garrett ducking into the casino and the pieces of the puzzle dropped slowly into place. "You owe him money, don't you? From gambling?"

"Stop talking." Garrett pushed the gun harder into Logan's temple. "I will kill him if I have to. Katie, I need you to untie Salvatore."

She was already shaking her head. No way. She couldn't do it. She just couldn't do it! Salvatore, now coming to, was watching the scene unfold, a satisfied smirk etched in his face. She tried one last time. "I can't believe you're turning your back on me, Garrett. And what about Dad? Did you have something to do with Dad's death, too?"

Garrett's face twisted in agony, but he didn't relinquish his hold on Logan. "Dad wasn't supposed to pull over Ravden. And Dad never works nights. He shouldn't have been there, just like you shouldn't be here now. There was nothing I could do. I didn't know Dad was a target until it was too late."

So her brother had known all along that their father was murdered. She fought the rising nausea. Would this nightmare never end? How could she get through to him?

Nick came closer, brushing ever-so-slightly against her. And belatedly she realized she still had the weapon she'd tucked into the back of her waistband. She took a tentative step sideways, turning enough to give Nick easier access to the gun.

But even as she stared at her brother, she knew

with a sick sense of certainty that it wasn't likely they would all make it out of this alive.

And she didn't know how to stop the ultimate destruction.

Logan couldn't stand watching Kate torment herself like this. He shouldn't have been so stupid as to get caught by Garrett in the first place. And he bitterly resented being used as a hostage.

He tried to catch Kate's gaze in an attempt to communicate what he wanted her to do, but she avoided looking at him. She was pale, her eyes wide with horror as she stared at her brother. He swallowed a helpless fury. The last thing he wanted was for her to untie Salvatore. Right now the odds were in their favor, three to one.

The situation would be better if Garrett wasn't holding a gun to his head, but he was deeply relieved that Kate wasn't the one he'd grabbed.

Please, Lord, keep Kate safe!

A movement caught his eye and he glanced at Nick, who was now standing directly behind Kate. For a moment he could only stare in shock. Anger radiated through him. What was Butler thinking to use Kate as a shield? He should be protecting her. Just because Garrett was her brother didn't mean she wasn't in grave danger.

He glared at Nick and saw his arm move, just a bit, as if he were reaching for something. What was he doing? Then he remembered—Kate had still had her gun before going over to make sure Russo was dead.

Nick was going to even up the odds, by getting Kate's weapon.

"Killing me isn't going to get you what you want," he said in an attempt to draw away Garrett's attention from Nick and Kate. "We can protect you through the witness protection program. Salvatore won't get his pound of flesh from you, unless you give it to him voluntarily."

"What good is witness protection?" Garrett asked harshly. "I'll lose everything, my family, my friends."

"And you think you won't lose them if you let Salvatore go?" he asked quietly. "Kate and your other brothers will become targets, just like your father was. Is that what you want? The only difference with you going into witness protection is that the rest of your family will be alive and safe from harm."

Was it his imagination or had Garrett loosened his hold? They couldn't afford to wait much longer—frankly he was surprised more of Salvatore's goons hadn't come looking for him yet.

Somehow, he needed Garrett to loosen his grip enough that he could get out of this.

"Don't listen to him," Salvatore growled, speaking up for the first time. "I'll find you no matter where you run and hide. And I'll find your family, too. I'm the only one who can keep you alive. If you try anything else, you and your family will die an ugly, slow, painful death."

There was a long pause as Salvatore's words sank deep, but surprisingly, Garrett's hold loosened even more and Logan glanced at Nick, knowing it was now or never. Nick flashed a barely perceptive nod and Logan abruptly twisted in Garrett's grasp, using both his hands to push Garrett's gun hand up and away from Logan's head. Garrett didn't go down easily, but struggled against him.

The sound of gunfire shattered the night.

Logan was suddenly free and he staggered back, trying to catch his balance. And then Garrett shocked him again, by turning and aiming his gun at Salvatore.

"No!" Kate cried at the same instant Garrett fired point-blank at Salvatore.

"Drop your weapon!" Nick shouted. Garrett didn't listen and Logan rushed him, hitting him in the center of his gut and pushing him backward.

Garrett's breath whooshed from his lungs, but he still held the gun, and it went off again before Logan could wrestle it away.

There was a cry of pain from behind Logan, but he didn't dare take his eyes off Garrett. He grabbed the guy's wrist and smacked it against the ground until he opened his fingers, letting go of the weapon. Logan snatched the gun and jumped to his feet, placing one squarely in the middle of Garrett's back, glancing behind him even as he pointed the weapon directly at Garrett. "Everyone okay?"

"Except for Salvatore. He's dead," Nick said, coming forward with another harness he'd taken from the wall of the tack room after he'd checked Salvatore's pulse and found none. He pulled together Garrett's hands behind his back and began tying him securely.

"Kate?" Logan tossed a worried glance in her direction, when she just stood there staring in horror at her brother. His heart twisted in his chest. She looked so forlorn. So shattered. He ached for her. "Hey, it's okay, Kate. We're safe. Everything is going to be fine." He didn't dare loosen his grip on the gun, not until he knew Nick had finished securing her brother.

"I have him," Nick said, tightening the harness around Garrett's wrists. "Call your boss because we're going to need help sorting all this out."

He wasn't quite ready to call Ken Simmons yet, not until he knew for sure who he could trust, but he took a deep breath and stepped back, lowering his gun. It was over. They didn't have the satisfaction of arresting Salvatore and Russo for their crimes, as both men were dead. But at least they were safe.

Kate was deathly pale and swaying on her feet.

He frowned and crossed over to put his arm around her. "Kate? What's wrong? Are you all right?"

"I don't think so," she whispered right before her knees buckled, and she collapsed against him.

He held her close, preventing her from hitting the floor. Had the shock of her brother killing Salvatore been too much to handle?

Gently, he lowered her to the ground. It took him a minute to see the blood seeping down her arm, and reality hit hard. Kate had been shot!

Cold. She was so cold. The pain in her shoulder was barely noticeable compared to the coldness seeping through her muscles. Spreading into her heart.

Reaching down to her soul.

"Kate? Don't you dare give up on me." Logan's terse voice penetrated the coldness. "The ambulance is on its way, so you need to hang on. Can you hear me, Kate? You need to hang on!"

She tried to shake her head, but it was too heavy. The coldness was everywhere now, making it impossible to move. Truthfully, she wasn't sure she wanted to fight against the sensation. Logan didn't understand, and she didn't have the energy to explain how the pain and the coldness was exactly what she deserved.

Forgive me, Lord. Forgive me for not seeing the

truth about Garrett. And forgive me for not stopping him sooner.

"Here, put this over her."

"Are you crazy? That's a horse blanket. She'll get an infection."

"She's going into shock, Logan. You have to keep her warm."

Something heavy was draped over her, surrounding her with the smell of horses. Strange, it wasn't as unpleasant as it had been earlier.

Or maybe she was losing her sense of smell. *Dear Lord, I'm ready to come home. Let Thy will be done.*

"Kate, please don't leave me." Logan's voice in her ear was full of worry. "I love you, Kate. Do you hear me? You have to fight for us."

Fight? Love? No, that couldn't be right. Her last conscious thought was that she didn't deserve Logan's love.

Logan was never so glad to see the paramedics, followed closely by several squad cars. "Save her," he said frantically as they rushed over with their gurney and the bag of medical supplies. "Hurry! She's already lost too much blood."

He could feel Butler's hand on his shoulder urging him backward, and he obliged, moving enough to give the paramedics access to Kate. But he wasn't leaving. Not until he knew she was going to make it.

"Do you have IV access yet?" the first paramedic asked.

"Yeah, I'll start fluids wide-open."

"Better add some O-neg blood, too. Her pulse is weak and thready."

"Gotcha."

The moment the paramedics had Kate's condition stabilized they lifted her onto the gurney and strapped her in. In some part of his mind, he heard Nick talking to the officers who'd arrived at the scene, but he didn't care. All he cared about right now was Kate.

"Logan, the officers here need your statement," Nick said, grabbing his arm as he started to follow Kate into the ambulance.

"Not now." Rudely, he shook off Nick's hand. "I'm going to the hospital with Kate."

One of the officers sputtered with anger. "Oh, no, you don't. You can't leave, I've got two dead bodies here and I need to know what happened!"

"Logan, she's in good hands," Nick said in a low voice. "They're not going to let you into the trauma room anyway. I'll drive you to the hospital as soon as we're finished here. We need to make sure we take care of this mess first, okay?"

No! He didn't want her to leave without him. But logically he knew Nick was right. Sitting in the waiting room of the E.R. wasn't going to help. The paramedics lifted Kate inside the ambulance and then climbed in after her, shutting the door behind them.

He shoved a frustrated hand over his hair and spun away from the ambulance, glaring at Garrett Townsend, Kate's brother, who was responsible for shooting her. By accident, maybe, but the end result was the same. Kate's brother refused to meet his gaze, but simply sat there, with his shoulders slumped as if he didn't care what happened to him any longer.

"I need your statement about what happened here," the annoyed cop repeated, breaking into his thoughts.

"Why don't you just play the tape?" Logan asked wearily.

The cop's jaw dropped. "Tape? What tape?"

If Kate's life wasn't hanging by a thread in the ambulance that was right now rushing her to the closest hospital, he might have smiled. As it was, he could barely manage a tight grimace. "Here, I'll show you."

The cops followed him from the tack room and into the empty horse stall on the other side. Walking over to the corner, he hunkered down and brushed the pile of straw out of the way. "Right here. We recorded everything from the very beginning."

The cops exchanged an incredulous look. The

annoyed cop wasn't going to give in that easily, though. "I still want your statement, and then we can compare everything to the taped version."

He sighed, irritated beyond belief at the cop's stubborn insistence. He didn't want to stand around here rehashing everything that had happened tonight. He wanted to get to the hospital to check on Kate.

"Logan, why not just call the head of your task force?" Nick asked in a low voice. "I'm sure your boss can pull rank over these guys and get you out of here."

"Not yet," he murmured. There wasn't time to tell Nick that he'd set up a meeting with his boss, only to be ambushed by a pretend homeless guy who'd tried to kill him.

Unfortunately he didn't know who to trust. And he didn't have time to figure it out now. Every instinct in his body wanted to get him to the hospital as soon as humanly possible. He desperately needed to know how Kate was doing.

The best way to get out of here was to cooperate, he realized abruptly. He turned and pinned the annoyed cop with a sharp gaze. "Fine, let's get this over with."

The cop headed to his squad car, leaving Logan to follow. As clearly and concisely as possible, he explained how he'd set up a trap for Salvatore to buy the listening device. He talked for almost fifteen minutes straight.

"You're a Feeb?" the cop asked with a smirk.

His jaw tightened with annoyance at the detested nickname. Local cops never appreciated the Feds taking over their turf. "Yes." He rattled off his badge number and then rose to his feet. "That's all I'm able to tell you for now. I need to get to the hospital and touch base with my boss. I'm sure we'll be able to fill you in on the rest later."

Apparently his story matched Nick's, because this time, the annoyed cop didn't stop Logan as he strode determinedly toward his friend. "Let's go."

Nick nodded in agreement. But before they took more than two steps, he stopped abruptly when a trio of men emerged from the darkness, heading straight toward them.

Of course, he recognized them immediately. His boss, Ken Simmons, led the way, flanked by Jerry Kahler, the man who'd come to meet him at the park only to take off when the bullets started flying, and Steven Johnson, the second-in-command to Simmons.

A cold chill snaked down his back.

What were they doing here? He hadn't called them, and no one else here would have known to make the call, either.

He stood stiffly beside Nick Butler, staring at the

three familiar faces, knowing his life depended on figuring out which one was the leak who'd set him up at the park in order to kill him.

SEVENTEEN

"What's going on here, Quail?" Ken Simmons snapped as they approached.

Logan tried to cover up the deep sense of foreboding as he faced his boss. "Actually, I was just about to call you. Since I haven't made the call yet, I'm wondering how you knew to come here."

Simmons scowled deeply at the challenging note in his voice. "When we heard about a gunshot wound here at the racetrack we decided to come and see for ourselves what was going on. Obviously you're not the one with a gunshot wound, so who is?"

We? Logan ignored his boss's question as he swept his gaze over both Jerry Kahler and Steven Johnson. He wanted to trust Simmons, but truthfully the leak could be any of the three. Or someone else entirely, although his instincts warned that one of the three men in front of him was the culprit.

"You were listening to a police scanner tuned in to this district?" he asked without bothering to hide his doubt. His boss wasn't one to interact with the locals.

Simmons turned to look at his second-in-command, Steven Johnson. After a brief pause the man responded. "I happened to be on the phone with Lieutenant O'Sabin, and he mentioned the call. I immediately reported the information to Ken and here we are."

Logan nodded, even as he tried to remember where he'd heard the name O'Sabin. There was something, just vaguely out of reach. All his instincts went on alert. Where had he heard that name before?

Suddenly, the memory clicked into place. Lieutenant Daniel O'Sabin was Kate's father's boss, the one she had talked to regarding her suspicions that her father's death was murder. His mind raced. Burke Townsend had worked out of a precinct in Chicago, which meant O'Sabin didn't have any jurisdiction here, forty-five miles outside of Chicago.

And O'Sabin wouldn't have overheard any chatter on the scanner about what was going down here, unless Garrett or some other dirty cop had tipped him off.

"I see," Logan drawled, considering his options. "Well, then, you should probably hear the whole story, right, Nick?" Logan glanced at the detective, trying to send a wordless warning. He needed to stall, needed time to think this through. If Johnson knew that both Russo and Salvatore were dead, then he'd get off scot-free. Somehow they needed to prove Johnson was actually working with the mob, before announcing the leader and his right-hand thug were now dead.

Nick looked puzzled, but apparently decided to play along. He leaned to the right, as if favoring his left leg. "Yeah, okay. But can we sit somewhere? My leg is killing me."

"Your leg?" Simmons asked, glancing sharply at Butler's jean-clad legs. "Are you the one who was shot?"

With the lights from the police car behind them lighting up the area, it didn't pay to fake a gunshot wound. "No, I wasn't shot. Just took a kick to the kneecap."

"So who was shot?" Simmons demanded irritably.

Logan lifted a hand. "It's a long story and I'll explain everything," he promised. "Let's head up to the racetrack. There's a private conference room inside that we can use without being disturbed."

"Fine." Simmons didn't look pleased, but he didn't argue. Logan gratefully swept past the three federal agents, leading the way to the main building housing the casino and racetrack. The farther he could take them from the crime scene, the better.

The backside of his neck tingled, and it took all his willpower not to turn and glance at the men following behind him. He imagined Steven Johnson was staring a hole through the center of his back. He seemed to be walking slow; was it possible he was injured? Maybe Johnson had either been the fake homeless guy or the man who'd followed them after church?

As they walked, he came up with a quick plan. He wanted to clue in Butler, so he bumped against him, knocking the detective off balance.

With an Oscar-winning performance, Butler groaned and sagged to the ground, as if his knee had given out on him. Logan quickly bent down to help him up. "Johnson's dirty," he whispered directly into his ear. Then louder, he said, "Sorry about that, are you all right?"

"Anyone ever tell you that you're clumsy?" Butler said with heavy sarcasm. He took Logan's arm to get back on his feet, but then shook it off. "I can walk."

"If you're sure," Logan said as they approached the building. He held open the door for Butler and the three federal agents. "This way," he said, leading the way through the building to the conference room.

It wasn't locked, and no one spoke until everyone was seated around the table. Everyone except Logan. He stood, positioning himself directly across from Johnson, who was seated right next to Nick Butler.

"As you already know, my cover was blown, but I still set up a sting operation to sell Bernardo Salvatore our surveillance technology," he said, starting from the beginning and hoping that Butler had his gun trained on Johnson. "I had been listening to Salvatore's private conversations with Congressman George Stayman, which helped Salvatore believe me about the technology."

"Congressman Stayman?" Simmons echoed with a feral gleam of anticipation in his eyes. "Did he say anything incriminating?"

He nodded, filling them in on the money and the fixed race. "But that's not all I overheard. Seems as if Salvatore has a federal agent on his payroll, as well."

"What are you talking about?" Simmons asked harshly, the look of shock seemed real enough. "That's impossible."

"Is it?" Logan glanced at Kahler, who was seated across from Simmons. Jerry Kahler shifted uncomfortably in his seat, as if remembering what happened at the park. "Russo is dead," Logan continued, "but we managed to get Salvatore alive. He told us about the leak from inside the task force. Didn't he, Butler?"

"Yes, he did." Butler smirked as he played along with Logan's story, and Logan could see from the position of his shooting arm that he had his gun trained directly on Johnson under the table.

"Not very smart of you, Johnson," Logan drawled. "Salvatore gave you up, and even if he hadn't talked, I know that Lieutenant Daniel O'Sabin was Burke Townsend's boss. He's in Chicago's fifth district, without any jurisdiction here. Which means you couldn't have talked to him, unless one of his dirty cops clued him in. You sold me out that day I went to the park, didn't you?"

"Don't be ridiculous," Johnson snapped, although a hint of sheer panic shadowed his eyes. "You don't have a shred of proof."

"Oh, but we do," Logan said smoothly, hoping to wring a confession out of the man. "I told you we have Salvatore in custody. Why don't you tell us your side of the story? Otherwise we'll have no choice but to listen to his version."

By now, Simmons was glaring at Johnson, as if he was starting to believe Logan. "You told me O'Sabin was a lieutenant on the police force here."

"I made a mistake, so what?" Fear was beginning to ooze like sweat from Johnson's pores. "Whatever Salvatore told you is a lie. I wouldn't work for that scumbag."

"But you did," Logan countered. "It was you who told Salvatore about how Burke's daughter, Kate Townsend, was poking her nose into the circumstances around her father's death. It was you who instructed Salvatore and Russo to get rid of her. Wasn't it?"

Johnson shoved away from the table and leaped to his feet, but Butler was there, pointing his weapon at the center of his chest. "One move and you're a dead man," he said quietly.

There was a tense moment, before Johnson caved. "All right! Salvatore was blackmailing me," Johnson said, then suddenly dropped into his chair in defeat. "He threatened to kill my wife and my two daughters if I didn't feed him information. I only told him enough to make him think I was playing along. I didn't tell him hardly anything! And I didn't have a choice!"

For a moment, Logan couldn't believe he'd managed to get the confession. "You set me up to be killed, didn't you?" he asked again.

"Yes. I sent a dirty cop to follow you and to meet you at the park, but I also sent Kahler to help you," Johnson admitted. "You don't understand, he threatened to kill my whole family."

Logan took a deep breath and let it out slowly. They had him. This part of the nightmare was finally over. Salvatore and Russo were both dead. They had one dirty cop, Garrett, in custody. Now they had the leak in the FBI task force plugged. His work here was done.

"I need to get to the hospital," he said, looking at his boss. "The gunshot victim is Kate Townsend, and I need to know how she's doing."

Simmons nodded. Nick tossed a set of handcuffs

at Kahler, who didn't hesitate to secure Johnson's wrists. The minute they were finished, Nick holstered his gun and turned to Logan. "Let's go."

He took off running for the SUV, urgency driving him to get to Kate as soon as possible. Nick was hot on his heels and slid into the driver's seat. As Nick drove to the hospital, Logan sat in the passenger seat and prayed that God would be merciful, sparing Kate's life.

The sharp scent of antiseptic pierced Kate's subconscious. Gradually, she became aware of her surroundings.

She could hear the murmur of voices, but couldn't understand what was being said. Her eyelids were too heavy to lift, although she could tell there were bright lights on overhead. The coldness that she remembered was gone, although now she could feel pain, mostly in her left shoulder.

With an effort, she tried to move her arms and her legs, even though that only made the pain worse.

"She's waking up," a deep voice said from beside her. "Kate? Open your eyes for me. Please?"

She tried to do as the voice asked, but the lights were too bright, forcing her to squeeze her eyelids tightly.

As if the person beside her bed had read her mind, the bright lights were abruptly turned off.

"Try again, Kate," the deep voice said again. "Open your eyes for me. I'm here for you."

She could feel a warm hand clutching hers and the memories clicked into place. Logan. Held at gunpoint by her brother Garrett. Logan's arms catching her as she fell. The way he told her that he loved her.

She should feel something in return, shouldn't she? But all she felt was emptiness.

"Everything's fine, Kate," Logan said softly. "You had surgery on your shoulder, but the damage wasn't too bad. You're safe now. Salvatore and Russo are both dead."

She knew that, remembered the events from the tack room with Technicolor clarity. She forced open her eyelids and immediately saw Logan's face hovering above hers, his tawny gaze full of worry. But then the corners of his eyes crinkled as he smiled. "There you are. I've been waiting for you to show me those Irish-mud eyes of yours," he whispered huskily.

Irish-mud eyes, just like her father's. And Garrett's. The thought of her brother filled her with sadness. "I'm sorry," she croaked, her throat dry and scratchy.

"You don't have anything to apologize for, Kate," he murmured, staring down at her with relief mixed with wonder. "Do you want some water? They said you could have a couple sips when you woke up."

"Yes." Logan's face moved out of her line of vision as he reached to pick up a glass. He pushed the button on her bed, raising the upper half enough so that she wouldn't choke, before he held out the cup and straw.

"Slowly, now," he cautioned. She took a tentative sip and savored the coolness on her sore throat. After a few more sips, Logan gently took away the cup. "Easy, you don't want to be sick."

"No," she agreed. The water seemed to have infused strength as well, because she was able to glance around the room curiously.

"You're in a room on the surgical floor," he said, answering her unspoken question. "You had surgery last night, and now it's ten o'clock the following morning."

She'd managed to lose twelve hours, but figured it could have been worse. She was alive. Apparently God hadn't taken her after all. She knew that meant God had a plan for her, but she was too tired to try to figure out what that plan might be. It seemed as if her whole life had fallen apart, lying in tatters at her feet. Everything she'd once had seemed to be gone, forever.

"Garrett?" she asked, bracing herself for Logan's anger. Not that she could blame him. It was her fault that her brother had found them.

"He's in custody," Logan said gently. "And he's cooperating fully, telling the police and the FBI everything he knows about Salvatore's operation. He's confessed to every single one of his crimes. And apparently, he gave Angela Giordano money to disappear. So she's safe, not dead the way we feared."

"I'm glad," she said huskily, fighting tears. At least Garrett had tried to do that much. Part of her wanted to be with her brother, supporting him through this, yet there was another part of her that was disgusted with his choices. How could he have sold out to Salvatore? She wondered if his marriage had broken up because of his gambling. Guilt seared through her that she hadn't known about his problem. A problem that had led him so astray, he'd inadvertently caused their father's death. She knew she needed to find a way to forgive him, but it wasn't going to be easy.

Please, Lord, help me find a way to forgive Garrett.

Logan took her hand again, and she didn't have the strength to pull away. "Kate, it's over. Salvatore's operation is going down. We may not get everyone involved, but we've made a big enough hole in his organization that the ones who are left will scatter like roaches. There was a guy from inside the FBI task force working with Salvatore, but we got him, too."

"That's good," she murmured. Her eyelids were

starting to feel heavy again, and she blinked, trying to pry them back open.

"Rest now," he crooned. "You need to build up your strength."

She gave in to the overwhelming exhaustion layered with pain medication, even though she knew there was something she needed to tell Logan.

Something important. But for the life of her, she couldn't remember what it was.

The next time Kate opened her eyes, there were two men in her room, and she almost wept with relief when she saw the familiar faces of Sloan and Ian, her middle brothers.

"Katie? How are you, sis?" Sloan was on the right side of her bed, while Ian hovered on the left.

"Okay," she whispered, even though she really wasn't. But she couldn't deny being happy to see them, and wondered if this was Logan's doing.

For a moment she considered how things might have gone down if she'd called either Ian or Sloan rather than Garrett the night Angie had called. Probably very differently. But it was useless to play the what-if game, so she thrust aside the thought.

"We heard about everything from your cowboy federal agent," Sloan said, his dark brown eyes full of concern and reproach. "You should have called us. We would have kept you safe."

She didn't have the energy to explain why she

hadn't called them. At the time, keeping her family as far from Salvatore as possible had been her priority, but now she felt foolish. Easy to understand why her brothers were upset with her. "I'm sorry."

Ian and Sloan looked at each other, but she must have looked pathetic enough that they didn't pursue the issue. "Do you need something for pain?" Ian asked.

Her shoulder felt as if it was on fire, but she shook her head. She didn't like feeling fuzzy and incoherent. "Water," she croaked.

Awkwardly, Ian held up the cup of water so she could take a sip. Idly, she wondered where Logan was. It was nice of him to get her brothers to sit with her, when he'd obviously needed to go back to work. Hadn't he said something about a guy inside the task force being in league with Salvatore? Logan would be tied up for a long time. Days. Weeks. Maybe longer.

The thought of never seeing Logan again hurt worse than her shoulder.

Yet at the same time, she knew that pushing him away was the only option. She'd failed him. In so many ways. She still couldn't get over how her eldest brother had almost killed him. And worse, the moment Garrett had grabbed him, she'd frozen in place. No matter how much she cared about

Logan, she didn't think she'd have been able to pull the trigger on her own brother.

She'd wanted Logan to treat her as a partner, but instead she'd been a liability. She had a degree in criminal justice, but with her injury, she couldn't try out for the academy. Even if she wanted to.

Which she didn't.

A tear slipped out from the corner of her eye, trailing down her cheek. She normally hated people who had their own pity party, but somehow she couldn't manage to pull it together. For so long, she wanted to be loved for who she was, yet she didn't know who she was anymore.

All she knew was that she didn't have anything to offer Logan. Nothing but a shell of the woman she'd once thought she was.

"Katie, don't cry," Ian begged. "We're here for you. You can stay with one of us when you're ready to bust out of here."

She wiped away the moisture with her hand of her uninjured arm and tried to smile. She had to reassure her brothers, or they'd camp out here and never leave her alone. "I'm fine. Just tired."

After all, there was no cure for a broken heart.

EIGHTEEN

By the next morning, Kate felt much more human. Her shoulder still hurt like crazy, especially when the physical therapist, better known as the torture specialist, made her move her injured arm, but all in all, she'd recovered from surgery without a problem.

Her brothers had finally left her alone, and while she missed them, she was also grateful to have some breathing room. She decided right then and there to go back to her old apartment once she was discharged, rather than live with one of them. She needed time and space to figure out who she was now that she knew she could no longer qualify as a cop.

She was sitting in the chair beside her bed, waiting for the pain meds to kick in once the therapist had left, when she heard a sharp knock on her door. "Come in," she called, expecting the doctor, since he'd talked about discharging her within a day or two.

But to her shocked surprise, it was Logan who

walked in. "Hi," he said with a warm smile. "You look tons better than the last time I saw you."

"Yeah, I'm great." Well, not really great, but good enough. She ignored the dark thoughts. "How is everything with the task force?"

He shrugged. "It'll be busy for a while yet, mostly because of Johnson." At her puzzled look, he added, "The second-in-command who was being blackmailed by Salvatore."

"I bet." She couldn't begin to imagine the mess Logan had left behind in order to come see her. She took a deep breath and let it out slowly. "I need to thank you, Logan, for saving my life."

He sat down on the edge of her empty hospital bed so he could face her. "I'm the one who should be thanking you," he corrected softly. "The way you kept your brother talking was brilliant."

She narrowed her gaze, trying to figure out if he was joking. "If it hadn't been for my brother, your life wouldn't have been in danger at all."

Logan grimaced. "I'm not proud of the way he managed to get the drop on me. It was my own stupidity that got me in trouble, Kate. You're the one who saved me."

He was just saying that to be nice. And suddenly she was overcome with a flash of anger. "Just stop it, Logan. You were right. I'm not cut out to be a cop. All my life I wanted to be like my brothers and my dad…." She blinked, willing away the tears that threatened. "But obviously, that career path is over." And she'd have to figure out what to do with the rest of her life.

Figure out who she was.

She hadn't felt this lost since her mother had died.

"Kate, you're the strongest, smartest and most courageous woman I've ever known," Logan said, his steady gaze capturing hers. "You can do anything you want to. When you were injured, I realized just how much I love you. And I want you to know, I will support you, no matter what career path you decide to choose."

The *L* word distracted her. She'd cared about him for so long, even though he was irritatingly protective. But that was when she had something to offer. Now she had nothing. She was still an empty, useless shell. "I don't know what to say," she whispered. "I'm sorry, Logan, but I can't love you the way you deserve to be loved."

For a moment, his eyes darkened with what almost looked like panic. "What are you talking about? I know you care about me."

She couldn't lie to him. "I do care about you, Logan. That hasn't changed. But I can't give you what you need. Not now."

And maybe not ever.

Logan couldn't believe that Kate had sent him away. He stood propped against the wall outside her hospital room, trying to figure out what had gone wrong. He'd told her that he loved her and he'd been fairly certain that she'd felt something for him, too. He hadn't imagined her response to his kiss, had he?

Frustrated and feeling helpless, he scrubbed the back of his neck beneath the brim of his cowboy hat. Just as he was about to push away and leave, he caught sight of her brothers walking toward him.

"What's the matter, cowboy?" Kate's brothers looked similar enough to be twins, but he'd already figured out that Ian was slightly taller and leaner than Sloan. "You look like you lost your best friend."

Because I did, he thought bleakly. "Kate will be happy to see you," he said instead.

The brothers exchanged a long look. "Nah, we tend to get on her nerves," Ian said.

"Yeah, and she's already talking about going back to her apartment, rather than bunking with one of us," Sloan spoke up. "She's so stubborn, I doubt we can talk her out of it."

He thought briefly about taking her home to Texas, although he doubted she'd agree. He, along with his parents and his brother, would love to have her.

But her medical team was here, so taking off halfway across the country probably wasn't the best option.

He curled his fingers into helpless fists. "Don't let her go home alone," he said tightly. "I'd take her back home to my folks in Texas, but she'll need ongoing care, so you'll just have to make her go home with one of you. Understand?"

The brothers exchanged another long look. "I'm getting the impression you care about our baby sister," Sloan said slowly as Ian nodded thoughtfully.

There was no use in denying it. "Yeah, I'm in love with her. But right now, she doesn't seem to want anything to do with me." And for the life of him, he didn't know why.

"I hope you're not going to give up that easily?" Ian asked, crossing his arms over his chest. "Because our sister is worth fighting for."

"I'm not giving up," he murmured. "I just need a new battle plan."

Ian grinned and Sloan slapped him on the shoulder. "Good for you," Sloan said. "And we'll help, right, Ian?"

"Right."

Logan lifted a brow, his gaze wary, since he wasn't sure if they had the power to really help him or to just make things worse. And he suspected the latter.

"I'll take care of it myself," he said finally, pushing the brim of his hat farther back on his head.

"Go in to see her. I'll wait here until you're finished."

Kate's brothers looked as if they wanted to argue, but Sloan shrugged and Ian went to knock on the door. "Your funeral," Sloan muttered.

When the brothers disappeared inside Kate's room, he stayed where he was, thinking over everything that had happened in the ten days since Kate had reentered his life.

And he formulated his battle plan.

"For the last time, *no!*" Kate's patience with her loudmouthed, overbearing brothers was wearing very thin. Her shoulder was throbbing and she desperately wanted to crawl back into her bed. "I will not come home with either of you. End. Of. Discussion."

"Fine. Then you leave us no choice but to make other arrangements," Ian said, throwing her his best no-nonsense look.

She didn't have the energy to go round two with them. "I need to use the bathroom," she muttered, knowing it was the one place they couldn't follow.

Her brothers backed up comically. "Aah, sure. We'll get your nurse."

She stayed right where she was, closing her eyes as she rested her head against the pillow that was propped behind her back.

"Are you all right?"

She opened her eyes to find Logan standing there. And for the first time, she was extremely glad to see him, especially after the relentlessness of her brothers. "I'm fine. I'd be better if you'd kick out my brothers for me."

Logan's lips quirked in a lopsided smile. "I might do that, if you'll do something for me."

Instantly, her guard came back up. "What?"

"Come recuperate at my family's ranch, the Lazy Q. Allow my mother to fuss over you, treat you like the daughter she never had."

Her mouth dropped open. "Are you crazy?"

"Kate, I'm only crazy about you. I love you. And I understand you need time to recover from all this, but I know you care about me, too." He knelt in front of her so their eyes were level. "Please tell me you don't believe your career defines who you are?"

His question stabbed deep. Because he was exactly right. Her career had defined who she was. She'd wanted to be accepted for herself, for being the tough cop she'd wanted to be, but maybe she'd only been fooling herself. Logan's earlier words echoed through her mind. *You're the strongest, smartest and most courageous woman I've ever known. I will support you, no matter what career path you decide to choose.*

Stunned, she stared at him. "I don't know," she whispered. "But I think I have been doing just that."

"And I don't believe any career could define all

of you. And you know why I know that? Because you have faith. And you helped show me the way back to my faith. God has given you special gifts, Kate, and He has a plan for you. Isn't that what you've told me?" Logan's smile was sad. "Think about it, Kate. I'm offering you a chance to recuperate at my family's ranch, which will provide plenty of time for you to think about and pray about God's plan. Time to consider what you really want out of life."

"I couldn't," she whispered, even as the possibility turned around in her mind. Could she? The idea was far more tempting than it should be. If she'd been following the wrong path, then she needed time to understand what path she was to take.

"Sure you can. I spoke to your doctor and he said he'd make arrangements for you to have follow-up care, including physical therapy, at a hospital in Texas. I have some time off coming, so I'd be there to drive you back and forth. And my folks will be there, so you wouldn't ever be alone." Logan looked nervous, as if he was afraid of her answer. "Think about it, Kate. Just promise me you'll at least think about it."

"She'll do more than think about it," Sloan piped up from the doorway. She glanced past Logan to where both her brothers were standing, obviously having listened to every word. "She'll choose, won't you, Katie? You'll choose between staying with me and Ian, or going to Logan's ranch."

She narrowed her gaze, annoyed with the way her brothers always wanted to bulldoze over her feelings. "There's a third option, you know," she pointed out with a scowl.

"No, there isn't." Logan's tone was gentle yet firm. "You can't do this alone, Kate. You're the one who taught me the value of partnership, remember? I'm offering that same partnership opportunity to you now. Come home with me. My family will love you and my mother will help take care of you."

She bit her lip, knowing he was right. She couldn't manage everything on her own; she needed help. But the thought of going with Logan to his ranch, to live temporarily with his parents, for goodness' sake, was intimidating. Yet staying here with her brothers wasn't exactly appealing, either.

Staring up into Logan's eyes, she realized that he was right. She had been using her career to define herself as a person. Maybe being around men for so long, especially after her mother died, had made her lose sight of the fact that she was so much more.

If she were honest with herself, she would admit that she wanted to be a detective, solving puzzles and crimes, more than she really wanted to be a cop. But you had to be a cop first, before you could sit for the detective exam.

Plenty of time to figure that out later. Right now,

she needed to get healthy. "All right, Logan," she said quietly. "I'll go with you to your ranch, so I can recuperate. And pray for God to show me His way."

He blinked, and then a broad smile split his face. "Really?"

She couldn't help smiling back at him. "Yes, really." She reached out to take his hand. "I need you, Logan. I'm feeling a little lost at the moment, even though it helps to have you here with me."

"I need you, too, Kate. But I'm not feeling lost. I feel exhilarated. Like this is the beginning of something great."

Her heart swelled with emotion. And love. Suddenly, she didn't feel empty anymore. This was what God wanted her to understand. He'd brought Logan into her life to make her realize that she had so much more to offer. If she were strong enough to listen. And believe. She stared at Logan intently, unable to hold her feelings back any longer. "I love you, Logan. I'm sorry I didn't tell you earlier."

"There's no rush, Kate," he murmured, his fingers tightening around hers. "We have plenty of time. I want you to take as long as you need."

That made her smile, especially when she could see the goofy grins on her brothers' faces. "I don't need time to let you know how I feel," she said. "I love you and nothing is going to change that."

Logan gently leaned forward to give her a sweet kiss. "I'm glad to hear it," he whispered huskily.

"Well, I'm glad that's settled," Ian said, breaking the moment.

"Yeah, me, too," Sloan agreed with a smirk. "She's all yours, cowboy."

"Just don't hurt her, or we'll have to come find you," Ian added.

"And hurt you," Sloan piped up.

"He won't," Kate said confidently, raising her hand to cradle his cheek. How did she get so lucky to have this wonderful man come into her life? "And you both know full well I can take care of myself."

"That you can," Logan murmured. He kissed her again, this time lingering over her mouth, until she was breathless.

And she couldn't help being extremely glad when her brothers finally turned to go, leaving them alone.

So she could kiss Logan in private.

EPILOGUE

Two months later...

Kate was sitting in a lawn chair Logan had set up for her in a perfect spot to watch him and his younger brother, Austin, break in a new horse. She winced when Austin hit the dust for the second time in a row. He picked up his hat, swatted it against his thigh and put it on his head before heading determinedly back toward the horse.

Logan shook his head, and stood beside Austin, letting the horse trot off. Clearly, Logan thought the new colt had been through enough. Then he glanced over and headed toward her.

"Hey," she said, shading her eyes from the sun.

"Hey, yourself." Logan dropped his head to steal a kiss before he lowered himself onto the ground next to her. "My boss is due to arrive tomorrow," he said casually, as if he were discussing the weather.

She glanced at him in surprise, hiding a stab of disappointment. She knew Logan would have to go back to work eventually, but she'd been enjoying having him to herself. Well, along with the rest of his family. His mother had been nothing but wonderful. "Really? Vacation time over, huh?"

"Actually, it's not just me that he wants to see." Logan stretched out, propping himself up on his elbows. "He wants to talk to you, too. He's waiting for your answer."

She still hadn't quite comprehended that his boss wanted her to join the FBI. "What if I'm not sure yet?"

Logan tipped his head to the side and studied her from beneath his brim for several long moments. "Kate, I keep telling you that I'll support you in whatever you want to do. But before my boss gets here, I do have one question to ask."

"Oh, yeah? What's that?"

He rolled up so that he was kneeling beside her chair, holding out a small velvet ring box. "Will you marry me?"

"Marry you?" She couldn't help the surprised squeak in her tone. "Oh, Logan, are you sure?"

A smile played along the edge of his mouth. "I'm sure I love you. I'm sure I'll support whatever you want to do, whether it's stay home and have our babies, which is a top vote in my book, by the way, or whether you want to return to work for a while first. Your shoulder is almost healed, so it's really up to you."

She held out her hand so that he could slide the engagement ring on her finger. "Yes. I'll marry you. I'll have your children. And I'll love you for the rest of my life."

"Thank You, Lord," he muttered, before dragging her up out of the chair and into his arms. "I love you, Kate, so much."

"I love you, too." She kissed him, and then leaned back so she could look into his eyes. "As much as I want to have your children, I would also like to do something important with my life. I want to make a difference." In some weird way, she wanted to make up for Garrett's mistakes, although he was serving a reduced term due to the way he'd cooperated with the authorities.

"I know," he murmured, reaching up to tuck a strand of her hair behind her ear. "If you decide to join the bureau, after you finish your training, we can work together. As partners."

The idea was tempting. Ken Simmons had told her that, with her four-year degree in criminal justice, she had a good shot of getting in. "Partners?"

"Yes. I think we'd make a great team."

She felt a sense of completion. She'd spent the past eight weeks falling more deeply in love with Logan, renewing her faith and getting stronger physically. Logan had been at her side the entire time.

And suddenly, she knew that being his partner—

in every way—was exactly what she wanted. She leaned into his embrace. "I think you're absolutely right, Logan. Whether we're working together, or creating a family of our own, we make a great team."

"Career first, then babies," he murmured, before kissing her again.

And she kissed him back, agreeing with his timeline. Because she was willing to accept whatever God had in store for them.

* * * * *

Dear Reader,

I have the utmost respect for officers of the law, and once even considered trying out for the police academy. However I made do with my career in nursing, but my fascination with the men and women who uphold the law tends to spill over into my stories. You met Logan and Kate in *Twin Peril* and according to your emails, you've been patiently waiting for their story.

Kate comes from a long family of cops, and has made up her mind to join her father and her brothers by becoming a police officer. But her plans are interrupted when her father dies unexpectedly. Determined to prove his death was murder, she ends up being held at gunpoint by Salvatore's thug. Logan rushes to the rescue, even though it means blowing his cover.

Believing in God's plan is the theme of this book and I hope you enjoy reading Logan and Kate's story. I'm always thrilled and honored to hear from my readers and I can be reached through my website at www.laurascottbooks.com.

Yours in faith,
Laura Scott

Questions for Discussion

1. In the beginning of the story, Kate believes her former roommate, Angela, is in trouble. Please discuss a time when you believed someone who wasn't being truthful with you. Is there anything you would do differently? Why or why not?

2. Logan is forced to blow his cover in order to rescue Kate from Russo. He loses his temper as a result. Discuss a time you've gotten angry and how you handled it.

3. We learn Kate intends to become a cop, like her brothers, her father and her grandfather. Do you think women should be police officers or in the military? Discuss why or why not.

4. Kate is grieving her father's death just as Logan still grieves for his dead fiancée. Discuss how you may have coped with losing a loved one.

5. We soon realize Logan has lost his faith after his fiancée's murder. Discuss a point in your life when you let your faith lapse.

6. As Logan and Kate escape the gunman, Logan begins to pray. Discuss the time when you first

began to pray and how that may have changed your perspective on faith.

7. Kate tells Logan that God has a plan for him, but he isn't sure he believes her. Describe a time when you weren't sure what God's plan was for you and how you coped.

8. Kate wants to be loved for herself, not for the way others want her to be. Discuss a point where you felt you weren't accepted for the way you are.

9. Logan agrees to go to church with Kate, and hears a sermon on everlasting life. Discuss the first time you accepted Jesus and how that influenced your beliefs about life after death.

10. Toward the end of the story, Kate is betrayed by someone she loves. Discuss a time you were betrayed by someone you loved or discuss how Kate must have felt when she realized what happened.

11. Kate wants to support her brother yet at the same time she's angry with his choices. Discuss a time you felt the same way toward someone you loved.

12. Kate thinks she's defined by her career and Logan helps her to realize she's not. Discuss a time when faith helped you believe in yourself.

LARGER-PRINT BOOKS!

GET 2 FREE
LARGER-PRINT NOVELS
PLUS 2 FREE
MYSTERY GIFTS

Love Inspired®
SUSPENSE
RIVETING INSPIRATIONAL ROMANCE

Larger-print novels are now available...

YES! Please send me 2 FREE LARGER-PRINT Love Inspired® Suspense novels and my 2 FREE mystery gifts (gifts are worth about $10). After receiving them, if I don't wish to receive any more books, I can return the shipping statement marked "cancel." If I don't cancel, I will receive 4 brand-new novels every month and be billed just $4.99 per book in the U.S. or $5.49 per book in Canada. That's a savings of at least 23% off the cover price. It's quite a bargain! Shipping and handling is just 50¢ per book in the U.S. and 75¢ per book in Canada.* I understand that accepting the 2 free books and gifts places me under no obligation to buy anything. I can always return a shipment and cancel at any time. Even if I never buy another book, the two free books and gifts are mine to keep forever.

110/310 IDN FVZ7

Name	(PLEASE PRINT)	
Address		Apt. #
City	State/Prov.	Zip/Postal Code

Signature (if under 18, a parent or guardian must sign)

Mail to the Harlequin® Reader Service:
IN U.S.A.: P.O. Box 1867, Buffalo, NY 14240-1867
IN CANADA: P.O. Box 609, Fort Erie, Ontario L2A 5X3

**Are you a current subscriber to Love Inspired Suspense books
and want to receive the larger-print edition?
Call 1-800-873-8635 or visit www.ReaderService.com.**

* Terms and prices subject to change without notice. Prices do not include applicable taxes. Sales tax applicable in N.Y. Canadian residents will be charged applicable taxes. Offer not valid in Quebec. This offer is limited to one order per household. Not valid for current subscribers to Love Inspired Suspense larger print books. All orders subject to credit approval. Credit or debit balances in a customer's account(s) may be offset by any other outstanding balance owed by or to the customer. Please allow 4 to 6 weeks for delivery. Offer available while quantities last.

Your Privacy—The Harlequin® Reader Service is committed to protecting your privacy. Our Privacy Policy is available online at www.ReaderService.com or upon request from the Harlequin Reader Service.

We make a portion of our mailing list available to reputable third parties that offer products we believe may interest you. If you prefer that we not exchange your name with third parties, or if you wish to clarify or modify your communication preferences, please visit us at www.ReaderService.com/consumerschoice or write to us at Harlequin Reader Service Preference Service, P.O. Box 9062, Buffalo, NY 14269. Include your complete name and address.

LISLPDIR13

Love Inspired®

SUSPENSE

RIVETING INSPIRATIONAL ROMANCE

Watch for our series of edge-
of-your-seat suspense novels.
These contemporary tales
of intrigue and romance
feature Christian characters
facing challenges to their faith...
and their lives!

AVAILABLE IN REGULAR
& LARGER-PRINT FORMATS

For exciting stories that reflect traditional values,
visit:
www.ReaderService.com

LISUSDIR11B

ReaderService.com

Manage your account online!
- Review your order history
- Manage your payments
- Update your address

---

*We've designed
the Harlequin® Reader Service
website just for you.*

Enjoy all the features!

- Reader excerpts from any series
- Respond to mailings and special monthly offers
- Discover new series available to you
- Browse the Bonus Bucks catalog
- Share your feedback

Visit us at:

ReaderService.com

RS13